DARK AS NIGHT

A DCI DANI BEVAN NOVEL

BY

KATHERINE **PATHAK**

≈

THE GARANSAY PRESS

Books by Katherine Pathak

The Imogen and Hugh Croft Mysteries:

Aoife's Chariot

The Only Survivor

Lawful Death

The Woman Who Vanished

Memorial for the Dead
(Introducing DCI Dani Bevan)

The Ghost of Marchmont Hall

Short Stories:

Full Beam

DCI Dani Bevan novels:

Against A Dark Sky

On A Dark Sea

A Dark Shadow Falls

Dark As Night

The Garansay Press

This is a work of fiction. Names, characters, businesses, places, events and incidents are either the products of the author's imagination or used in a fictitious manner. Any resemblance to actual persons, living or dead, or actual events is purely coincidental.

All rights reserved. No part of this publication may be reproduced in any form or by any means - graphic, electronic, or mechanical, including photocopying, recording, taping or information storage and retrieval systems - without the prior permission in writing of the author and publishers.

The moral right of the author has been asserted.

© Katherine Pathak, 2015

#DarkAsNight

Edited by: The Currie Revisionists, 2015

© Cover photography Catacol Bay Images, 2015

PROLOGUE

The couple stood on a stretch of flat sand which seemed to spread out for miles into the distance. The pair were huddled in the shelter of a system of dunes, to protect them from the sharp easterly wind which was whipping across the deserted beach and out into the sea.

Holding the woman's hand tightly, the man said, 'why don't you come home with me? You know I love you and would take care of you.'

His companion kept her gaze fixed on a container ship, just visible along the horizon. 'What would be the point? I've got absolutely nothing to give.'

He put his gloved fingers up to her face, smoothing away the wayward strands of her straight, dark hair. 'I don't want anything from you. When are you going to understand that, my darling?'

She turned to look at him. 'Is that really true? How long will you be willing to wait for me to recover from this terrible state I'm in? You say it doesn't matter now, but in the months and years to come it will begin to.'

He shook his head violently. 'If you were with *me* then you wouldn't be so unwell. That is the truth of the matter and I *can* wait. You do me a disservice to suggest otherwise.'

The woman put out her arms and pulled him close. 'You are a good man, Rhodri. I know your words are genuine.' She tipped her face upwards and stared into his eyes. 'It's my daughter that I'm thinking of. I cannot walk out on her, whatever happens.'

Tears were slowly escaping onto the man's lined

cheeks. 'I would take her in too and love the girl as if she were my own.'

The woman nodded, as her body shuddered with sobs. 'Yes, I realise that you would. But she loves her father better than she loves me. For that reason I cannot ever leave them, because if I go it will mean leaving her behind forever.'

The man said nothing more. He simply held her to him, soothing his lover as she gently wept, hoping and praying there might be some way in the future that he could change her mind.

Chapter 1

DCI Bevan walked slowly around her office. At times, it was a bit like working in a goldfish bowl. Unless she pulled down the blinds, she could be observed from every single desk on the floor of the serious crime division.

It was late July. The sun was streaming in through the tall windows, making the building which housed the headquarters of Police Scotland stiflingly hot. Yet Dani was smiling as she inspected her domain. The senior detective was in her late thirties, lean and youthful, with a short crop of naturally dark hair. Bevan had only been a detective chief inspector for a couple of years. Now, she was contemplating another step up the ladder. Her performance in a recent case had brought her to the attention of the bosses upstairs. DCS Nicholson had suggested this was a good moment for the DCI to go for promotion, whilst Dani's star was in the ascendant.

A superintendent at City and Borders in Edinburgh was up for retirement. Nicholson had already suggested Bevan's name for the post. She probably only had a few months to decide. It could be many years before an opportunity like this one came up again for her. But Dani wouldn't find it easy. She had many friends in Glasgow. One in particular who she wasn't sure could manage in the job without her guidance.

As if on cue, DC Andy Calder appeared in the doorway, his one-time considerable girth transformed into upper body muscle. He grinned at his boss before entering the tiny room. 'Afternoon,

Ma'am. I've just finished the duty rota for the weekend. We seem to be fully manned.'

'Good. Nicholson has agreed to send in some bodies from central division to help us out. We'll need as many uniforms out there on the street as possible come Friday night.'

It was the final weekend in July, when the city celebrated the Glasgow Fair. This year, the council had revived the old practice of setting up stalls and a fairground on Glasgow Green. The festivities would culminate in a peaceful march through the streets of the city centre. As far as Dani was concerned, the entire venture amounted to a total policing nightmare.

'And you'll definitely be needing me for the whole weekend?' Andy looked almost gleeful at the prospect.

'Of course. I'll need everyone.'

Calder rubbed his hands together. 'I'm glad to hear it. Carol's mum wanted us to troop 'doon the watter' to her sister's place in Troon. They'll have to go without me now.'

'Would it really have been *that* bad to join them?'

'Oh, aye. Amy gets spoiled to bits and I'm completely surplus to requirements. My mother-in-law can have the job of putting her granddaughter to bed when she's had two days being pumped full with sweeties and ice-cream.'

'What about Carol, it can't be much fun for her either?'

'It's Carol's family though, isn't it? She's got a higher tolerance for them than I do. I'll make it up to her when they get back.' Calder turned on his heels and headed out to his workstation.

Dani watched him depart, hoping her friend wasn't being too blasé about the importance of this trip. She sighed. It made no difference anyway. The

DCI couldn't possibly have spared Andy this weekend. It was shaping up to be the busiest of the entire year.

*

Dani woke suddenly. Glancing at the bedside clock, she saw it was 2am. She levered herself up into a sitting position and swung her legs round to rest on the cold floor, recalling the vivid dream she'd just been having. It was about her mother.

Moira Bevan had committed suicide when Dani was eight years old. She'd been suffering from severe depression ever since giving birth to her daughter. There were never any more children. Moira had battled with alcoholism, a side effect of her condition, finally giving up the fight when she was only 37 years old. She took a handful of pills and washed them down with neat gin, just after her husband had left for work one morning.

Huw Bevan moved Dani away from the Welsh village where they'd lived as a family, a matter of months after his wife's death. Dani had never returned since. The memories were too painful.

Only very occasionally did Dani dream about her mum. Usually, it was if she had worries on her mind, due to work or relationship stress. The DCI suspected that on this occasion it was the prospect of policing the upcoming Glasgow Fair weekend which had prompted the spectre of Moira Bevan to return to her consciousness. Whatever the reason, the thoughts were unwelcome. She padded through to the kitchen and poured out a glass of water, leaning against the sink to drink it, staring out of the patio doors into the darkness shrouding her little garden.

There was only one photograph of Moira in the

house. When the glass was empty, Dani walked along the hallway to the front sitting room. She picked up the small frame which sat on the mantelpiece, noting how dusty it was. Pale blue eyes stared back at her from within a pale face, framed by perfectly straight, dark hair. Moira had been very beautiful.

For the first time in many years, the image before her evoked an immediate emotional response. Dani put up her hand to touch the tears which had begun to roll down her cheeks. Why she was experiencing such powerful feelings now, after so much time had passed, the detective had absolutely no idea.

Chapter 2

Glasgow Green, a park on the east side of the city, was milling with folk. It was early yet, but the stallholders were busy setting out their wares. Dani stood and watched as a huge fairground ride was wheeled up close to the concreted area which encircled the Doulton Fountain.

Calder strode across the dewy grass to join her. 'Should we cordon off the fountain, Ma'am? We don't want some drunk drowning in it later.'

'Good point. Can you ask a couple of uniforms to get onto it?'

Andy nodded.

The air was crisp and damp, but the orange tinted sunrise indicated it would be a very warm day. This incongruous swathe of greenery, positioned amongst the buildings and warehouses of the city, with dense rows of tenements and post-war housing just visible across this narrow section of the Clyde was the traditional home of the Glasgow Fair celebrations.

The DCI wouldn't usually object to a handful of merrymakers dipping their peely-wally, light deprived legs into the water of the Doulton Fountain, but today was different. There would be thousands of people on this green in a few hours. Dani couldn't risk anything going wrong.

She turned to her DC. 'We've got barriers up alongside the agreed route the marchers will take. We need to keep the crowds moving along Argyle Street at a brisk pace. They will stop and congregate in Princes Square. The traffic division are primed to close the road to vehicles between 12 and 3pm.'

Calder furrowed his brow. 'Let's just hope that everyone sticks to the agreed plan. Sunshine and alcohol have a strange effect on the good folk of Glasgow.'

Dani smiled thinly. 'Aye, so it does. But a strong police presence should help to calm things down.'

'What about the river? It has been known for the occasional idiot to jump off the St Andrew's suspension bridge in hot weather. A group of students did it a couple of years back.'

Bevan sighed. 'We'd better have a few men stationed over there, just in case. But it's a bloody big park. We can't possibly cover every inch of it.'

'No, Ma'am. We'll simply do what we can. The rest will have to be down to lady luck, I'm afraid.'

*

The mid afternoon sun was beating down mercilessly on the unmarked police van that DCI Bevan was standing next to. When she rested her hand on the sliding door to lean inside, Dani winced at the burning heat of the shiny black metal. 'Any sign of the girl, Gary?' She asked the young detective constable who was hunched up within. He was sweating in front of a monitor connected to CCTV cameras positioned at various points across the Green.

The man shook his head. 'There are thousands of people out there, Ma'am.'

Bevan sighed heavily, turning back towards the distraught couple who were propping each other up a few metres away, near to an overfilled litter bin encircled by wasps, though neither of the pair seemed to have noticed. She pushed back her sunglasses so that they rested on top of her head.

This way, the DCI could make proper eye contact when she spoke with them.

'I'm sorry, Mr and Mrs Hendricks, none of the cameras have picked up anything yet. But I promise that all our officers are on the lookout for Lily. Her description has been circulated.'

The woman put a hand up to her mouth, an expression of pure horror on her flushed, plump face.

'Just explain to me once again where it was that you lost contact with your daughter,' Dani said gently, more to distract the woman from her rising panic than for any other reason.

'Lily was badgering us for an ice cream, but the queue at the van was so long, we told her no. She was crying and refused to hold my hand,' Mr Hendricks explained. 'We turned away, to let her know we weren't going to give in to her tantrum. But when we turned back, she was gone.'

Dani considered how the Glasgow Fair weekend, in the centre of a packed field, wasn't perhaps the best of times to be practising your toddler taming techniques, but restrained herself from saying this out loud. 'Okay, most likely Lily has just got lost in the crowds. It happens quite frequently at events such as this. Please try to remain calm.'

Mrs Hendricks looked anything but and Dani sensed the woman was about to have some kind of emotional collapse, when the DCI spotted a uniformed WPC walking towards them, holding the hand of a little girl. She was wearing a red sundress that appeared at least a size too small for her.

'Is that Lily?' Dani immediately asked.

The DCI received no verbal reply. The couple immediately bolted towards the girl, wrenching Lily from the policewoman's grip and hauling her up into their arms.

The WPC continued in the direction of the van. When she was standing right next to her superior officer she lowered her voice and said, 'another family spotted the girl wandering around the fairground on her own. They brought her to where I was patrolling the main gate. Lily told me she was looking for her parents. She said they'd be in the beer tent, which is where she'd last seen them.'

'The Hendricks spun a different tale entirely. *They* said the girl had a tantrum because they wouldn't buy her an ice cream. In my experience, the kid is usually the one telling the truth.'

The mother turned and waved to Bevan, who nodded her head, indicating they were free to go.

'Shouldn't we inform social services?'

Bevan turned to address the policewoman, who she would have placed in her early twenties at most. 'There's no real evidence to go on. Besides, this little incident will have given the parents a wake-up call. The mum looked like she was about to collapse before you showed up with her daughter. Some people simply can't work out the consequences of their actions. They have to experience the worst in order to re-evaluate their decisions.'

'But they didn't experience the worst, did they?' The WPC swivelled round to stare hard at Bevan, her clear blue eyes bright and determined. 'Lily was returned to her mum and dad in the end, no harm done. Once the dust has settled, they'll soon forget. I suspect they've learnt no real lesson at all.'

The DCI did not reply, but glanced across and took note of the WPC's name and division, intending to look out for her in the future.

This young recruit's instincts were absolutely spot on.

Chapter 3

The light was fading to dusk when DC Andy Calder came to the end of his shift. The majority of the crowd who joined the march to Prince's Square had dissipated, drifting into the clubs and restaurants of the city centre.

The air hung thick and close as Calder took a final patrol along Argyle Street to Trongate. A few stragglers still remained, clinging on to one another and singing old tunes that Andy felt must have been composed well before any of them were born. Litter was strewn about the gutters, having collected there like scum around a plug hole. The sweeping machines would follow on later, cleaning up the city before the fun and games started up again the next day.

Calder radioed in to the Pitt Street Headquarters, letting them know he was heading back home. Carol and Amy had already left for the coast. Andy was aware there was no rush to return to the flat they shared off the Great Western Road. The detective decided to take a detour first, to drop in on a relative of his who he'd not been in touch with as much as he would have liked in the past few years.

When Calder drove into Paisley, it was nearly dark. He hoped it wasn't too late to make a social call. Mae Mortimer's house was an impressive Victorian villa in the suburb of Castlehead. It was a step up from the grey semi-detached ex-council property the woman had shared with Andy's uncle, when he'd still been around.

Mae Calder had re-married a couple of years

before. Her new husband ran a surveying company based in the centre of town. Andy didn't begrudge his aunt finding herself a decent bloke, but he was secretly glad that her children, Elizabeth and John, hadn't taken on Gavin's surname. Andy had called ahead and as he pulled his car onto the sloping driveway, Mae was standing inside the sandstone entrance to greet him.

A smile spread across his face as he approached her. Mae was 46 years old, tall and slim. Her reddish hair was neatly trimmed to frame her face and her make-up subtly applied. Mae was no longer the flame-haired beauty she'd been in her youth, but Andy noted how attractive she still was.

'Hi,' she called out in her sing-song voice. 'It's good to see you.'

Andy placed a kiss on both of her cheeks.

Mae led him inside. The hallway was wide and formal. The chequered tiles on the floor created a pathway through to a high ceilinged reception room, where Gavin and Lizzie were sitting on a long sofa in front of a giant television screen. Gavin immediately turned it off. Andy felt this action illustrated the class difference between them. In his parent's house, when visitors came, the telly stayed on.

The long-legged teenager jumped up and threw her arms around him. 'Uncle Andy! Mum didn't say you were coming!'

'It was a last minute thing,' Calder explained.

'How's Amy? I've seen the photos on Aunty Carol's Facebook page. She's absolutely gorgeous.'

'Aye, she's a bonny lassie. I'll bring her over the next time I come. They're away with Carol's mum right now, for the Fair weekend.'

The atmosphere became immediately tense after he uttered these words. Gavin broke the silence by putting out his hand to the detective. 'Andy. It's really good to see you again.'

Calder shook it firmly, nodding his agreement.

'Come on,' said Mae, leading him into an open-plan kitchen which lay beyond this room to the rear of the house. 'I'll make you a coffee and we can have a chat.'

Lizzie and Gavin remained in the sitting room, sensing that this conversation was intended to be private.

'Do you want coffee? Or something stronger, perhaps?' Mae busied herself rummaging in a cupboard, pulling down packets and jugs.

'A coffee would be perfect. I'm on duty for the whole weekend.' Andy perched on a stool up at the breakfast bar and watched her work.

Mae turned on her heels to glance at him, trying to look cheerful. 'Well, you would be. It's the busiest weekend of the year in Glasgow.'

'That's why I'm here,' Andy added quietly. 'I wanted to show you and the kids my support, but if me being around is awkward, then I won't stay long.' He tipped his head towards the sliding doors which separated them from the sitting room.

The woman didn't reply for a moment. Calder knew she was fighting with her emotions. 'No. We're pleased you stopped by. Gavin understands. It's important that we don't ever forget.'

Andy's uncle, Donald Calder had gone missing during the Glasgow Fair weekend in 2005. He was just 41 years old. The family had been living in a less salubrious suburb of Paisley back then. On the Saturday, Mae had woken up with a migraine. Donald had agreed to take the children, then 5 and 9 years old, to the fair in the city centre.

They'd all arrived back home at 5pm. Mae took a sleeping pill and a pain killer before bed and slept soundly until morning. When she awoke, Mae noticed that Donald wasn't beside her. It didn't look as if he'd come to bed at all. The police were called and a search made of the local area. No trace of Donald Calder was ever found. Mae felt the police always suspected he had another woman on the go and had run off with her. But within the Calder family, the belief was that Donald had gone out later that night and somehow ended up in White Cart Water, either by accident or design they weren't sure. A body was never recovered.

Mae set the coffee pot down on the bar between them. 'John's gone out tonight with his mates.' She lowered her head. 'It's him who finds the anniversaries the most difficult to cope with.'

'How is the lad enjoying university?' Andy added a dash of milk to his cup.

'He loves it. His halls of residence look out over Kelvingrove Park and he's close enough to bring his washing home at weekends.' Mae smiled. 'He's got a steady girlfriend now too. Shiona's a lovely lass.'

'How about Lizzie? She looks well.'

'Aye, but she's a homebody. It's been the same ever since her father disappeared. I have the opposite problem to most folk with teenagers. It's a battle to get her to go out with her friends, even for a burger in the High Street.'

'Has Lizzie ever been referred to a child psychologist? I've got some good contacts if you need a number?'

Mae sighed, the tiny lines fanning out from her eyes crinkling with concern. 'She did see someone, in the months after it happened. It helped for a while, but then the nervousness came back.' The woman gripped her mug tightly. 'It could simply be Lizzie's personality, you know. We can't blame everything on Donald going missing.'

'No,' Andy ventured. 'But it was a pretty

devastating event for the kids. Something like that is bound to have a lasting effect.'

Mae lifted a hand to her face and shuddered, as tears began to escape onto her cheeks. Andy stood up, coming round to place a hand on her shoulder. 'I'm sorry to bring it all back.'

The woman began to sob noisily. The anguished sound summoned Gavin into the doorway. He moved across the room and wrapped Mae in his arms, flashing Andy a hostile look as he did so.

When Andy left the Mortimers' place it was nearly midnight. They had arranged for him to bring Carol and Amy over for Sunday lunch in a couple of weeks. Mae had fully recovered her composure by the time their guest departed and she gave him a warm wave from the top of the steps as he backed out of the driveway.

Gavin Mortimer stood beside his wife, an arm placed firmly around her shoulders. His expression was much less cheerful. It was clear the man didn't relish the thought of Andy returning to their house any time soon and if the detective was honest, he could totally understand why.

Chapter 4

The Saturday passed without any major incidents. The lock-ups at the Holland Street station were full of drunk and disorderlies by midnight but the atmosphere was jolly enough.

On the following Sunday morning, Dani Bevan was taking her time to shower and dress. She wasn't due back at Pitt Street until 1pm. The DCI was daring to allow herself time to relax a little. After the revelries of the previous night, Bevan was expecting the city to be quiet today. There would be traffic problems certainly, as the many folk who'd headed down the coast for the weekend started to return, but this wasn't her jurisdiction. Another division could deal with that.

Dani popped a couple of slices into the toaster, lifting a mug of tea to her lips and savouring the warmth of the aromatic brew. Bevan experienced a shiver of anticipation as she considered that in less than seven days she would be seeing her boyfriend in Edinburgh, staying in his tiny apartment and enjoying a lazy Sunday morning like this one, lying in bed with him. The thought made her smile.

The sound of the telephone brought her back to the present. She put down her cup and moved swiftly into the hallway to answer it. 'DCI Bevan.'

'Morning Ma'am, it's Alice Mann here.'

'Good morning, Alice. Is there a problem?'

The detective constable hesitated. 'I'm not sure. There's only me and Dan Clifton in the department, so all emergency calls are being directed to us. I've just had a strange one. My instinct was to let you know about it immediately.'

Dani sighed. 'I'll finish my breakfast first, Alice. Then I'll be straight there.'

*

Andy Calder drove his boss out of Glasgow along the M77. In this direction, the route was reasonably clear. But on the other side of the central reservation, Bevan could observe the traffic gradually building to a standstill.

'When are Carol and Amy due back?' She glanced across at her companion, who had dark shades obscuring his eyes.

'Not until tomorrow. They didn't want to battle the Sunday queues.'

'Very wise. Carol needs to take advantage of the fact they've got the freedom to take these wee holidays. It will all change when Amy starts school.'

Calder swept the unmarked police car off the motorway and headed south-east, in the direction of East Kilbride. The address they were aiming for, in the suburban town of Giffnock, was already punched into the Sat Nav system. The directions led them through the quiet High Street and into a modern executive estate. The house that Andy pulled up outside was one of the larger properties, the front garden was well maintained and the grass lush and green, despite the recent heat-wave.

Jenny McLaren had opened the door before they reached the top step. Both officers held up their warrant cards.

'Please come inside,' the woman said quickly, ushering them into a square hallway which was dominated by a twisting staircase. A series of doors led off in various directions. Mrs McLaren took them through the one on the right, which conveyed them into a light sitting room with a bay window facing the front garden.

'Take a seat,' she added absent-mindedly, perching herself on the arm of the sofa.

Dani examined the woman's appearance closely. She was late forties, thin and wiry. Jenny McLaren had the physique of a runner and she wore her hair cropped short.

Calder pulled out his notebook. 'You called the police station at 7.30am this morning,' he began. 'You were concerned about your husband?'

'I'm more than concerned.' She glanced at a little gold carriage clock which sat on the mantelpiece above an electric fire. 'Nathan didn't come home last night. There's no message from him on the phone or email.'

'When did you last have contact with Mr McLaren?' Andy leant forward, feeling sweat begin to prickle beneath his stiff collar.

'Nathan took our boys to the Fair at Glasgow Green yesterday afternoon. We thought they might be too old for it, but they met up with a few of their friends and wandered about the stalls and rides for a while. The three of them were home just after seven. I'd left some food out but they'd eaten burgers from a stall.'

'You didn't go along with your husband and sons?' Dani prompted.

She shook her head. 'It wasn't really my kind of thing. Besides, I'm training for the Edinburgh Marathon next month, I needed to put some hours in yesterday.'

Bevan nodded with understanding. Her boyfriend James was also taking part in the race. It had dominated his every waking moment for the past few weeks.

'What happened after your husband returned home?' Andy felt an increasing sense of unease.

Jenny lifted her head and looked straight at him. 'The boys went up to their rooms. Nathan and I watched television in the snug for an hour or so but I wasn't feeling very well. I shouldn't have pushed myself so hard in the heat. I had an awful headache. I went up to bed at around 9pm. Nathan said he wouldn't be long himself.' Jenny paused, as a lump formed in her throat. 'That's what makes it so odd. When I woke in the morning he wasn't there beside me. I could tell he hadn't come to bed all night.'

'Had you taken a sedative of any description?' Andy enquired.

'No,' Jenny replied carefully. 'But I had a couple of Codeine tablets for my headache. They tend to knock me out.'

'Did Nathan know you'd taken a painkiller?' It was Bevan who asked this question.

Jenny looked bewildered, as if she had no idea where this line of inquiry was leading. 'I suppose I might have mentioned it, when I was heading up to bed. I honestly can't remember.'

'Okay. Are your sons at home?' Andy glanced out into the hallway. He could hear no sound of movement in the house.

Jenny's cheeks flushed. 'They're both in bed. That's what teenage boys do on a Sunday morning. I haven't told them their dad's missing yet. I'd like to do it myself.' The woman looked panicky.

Dani said gently, 'we wouldn't officially declare your husband missing at this stage. He is 52 years old with no health problems. Your husband has been away overnight somewhere without informing you. The traffic is awful around Glasgow right now. He may just have got held up trying to return home.'

Jenny's face became taut with anger. Bevan

noticed then that the woman had been quite badly sunburnt the previous day. 'You think Nathan's been in an all-night strip joint in Sauchiehall Street and now he's sleeping off his hangover in some tart's bed? You don't know my husband at all. He's a devoted family man. Nathan has *never* been away from home without telling us before. I don't care about the types of folk you usually deal with DCI Bevan. My Nathan is different to them.' She raised a thin finger and waggled it at the detectives. 'This is a missing persons' case and I demand it be treated as such.'

Chapter 5

'I don't know why Alice Mann thought this was a case for Serious Crime,' Bevan stated irritably, as she climbed back into the passenger seat and slammed the door shut. 'She's usually got such good instincts. The guy's clearly tried to have a night off from that old battle-axe and ended up oversleeping at his girlfriend's place. I hope he can come up with one hell of a decent cover story. I wouldn't fancy facing the wrath of Jenny McLaren.' Dani chuckled to herself, shooting a look at Calder, who she expected to be joining in with the joke.

Instead, the detective constable's face was totally impassive. Behind his dark glasses, Dani couldn't work out his mood at all.

Finally, once they'd manoeuvred their way out of the estate and merged into the slow-moving wall of traffic on the M77, Calder pushed his shades up onto the top of his head and cleared his throat. 'Ten years ago, on the Saturday of the Glasgow Fair weekend, a man from Paisley went missing. The scenario was very similar to the one we've just heard from Mrs McLaren. The man was called Donald Calder and he was 41 years old. He was my Da's wee brother. We've never heard from him since and the polis never found a body.'

Bevan shifted herself around to face him. 'I didn't know that, Andy. I'm really sorry. Did the police have a theory about what happened to your uncle?'

'Oh aye,' he chuckled dryly. 'It was something along pretty similar lines to the one you've just proposed for Nathan McLaren's disappearance.'

Dani cringed. 'I see. So I've finally become that

boorish, knuckle-headed copper stereotype we've always mocked, eh?'

Andy laughed, this time in better humour. 'If I didn't know about Uncle Donald's case then I'd be saying the exact same thing.'

Dani twisted back around and settled into her seat. 'Come on then, it looks like we're going to be in this jam for a good while yet. Why don't you tell me every single detail about the day Donald Calder went missing?'

*

By the time Bevan and Calder returned to the Pitt Street Headquarters it was late afternoon. The DCI called all the officers who were present to congregate around DS Phil Boag's workstation. There was by no means a full house. The team had been operating on a shift rota for the entire weekend. Many of the officers had already clocked off for the day.

Dani pulled across one of the flip charts and wrote Nathan McLaren's name in the centre of it. 'This man,' she prodded at the sheet with her felt tip, 'has been missing from his home in Giffnock since 9pm last night.'

One of the DCs at the back of the group raised his eyebrows and smirked.

'Aye, I know. Under normal circumstances we would be assuming that this chap was enjoying himself so much somewhere that he'd lost track of the time. But in this instance, I think we need to take it more seriously than that.' Bevan nodded towards Calder, indicating he should take over.

'McLaren spent most of yesterday on Glasgow Green, along with several thousand others. He was accompanying his two teenage sons. They are Cormac, aged 15, and Ewan, 17. The lads had arranged to meet up with friends from their High

School. His wife, Jenny, remained in Giffnock and ran a 15km course around the town. She's in training for the Edinburgh Marathon. We know that Nathan and his sons returned to their detached, five bedroom executive home at just after 7pm. Jenny McLaren last saw her husband when she went up to bed with a headache at 9pm. He's not been heard from since.'

'Any serious debts, or recent problems in the marriage?' Phil looked at his colleagues expectantly.

Andy shook his head. 'Nathan McLaren is a systems analyst at a financial services company based on York Street. Obviously, the offices are closed right now, but his wife scanned over their most recent bank statements. The figures look pretty healthy.'

'As for the state of the marriage,' Dani added. 'That's anyone's guess. I didn't warm much to the wife, but it could be the stress and worry making her cranky. I can't see Jenny McLaren opening up to us about marital disagreements willingly, though.'

'Even if it helps us to find her husband?' Alice Mann chipped in.

Dani shrugged her shoulders. 'The woman seems fairly highly strung.'

'We've had cameras set up all over the Green these past three days,' Phil interjected. 'There could be footage of Nathan. We might get a sense of what he and the boys got up to. I mean, if the teenagers were off with their mates, what did Mr McLaren do with his time?'

'Good idea. Can you sift through the footage, Phil?'

The DS nodded.

'So, why are we taking such an interest in this missing persons' case?' DC Alice Mann fixed her intelligent gaze upon the DCI. 'We wouldn't normally get involved in a domestic circumstance like this, unless a body had turned up.'

Dani allowed Calder to reply.

'On the 30th July 2005, my uncle, Donald Calder, accompanied his two young children to the fair on Glasgow Green. His wife, Mae, was suffering from a migraine and stayed at home. Donald and the kids returned to the family house in Paisley at just after five. Like Jenny McLaren, Mae had taken painkillers *and* a sedative before retiring early to bed.

When my aunt woke up the following morning, Donald was gone. He'd never come to the marital bed that night. The entire Paisley area was scoured for signs of him and appeals made on local radio and even on Crime Scotland in the days and weeks that followed. No trace of my uncle was ever found, not even a body.'

This information was greeted by silence.

After several uncomfortable minutes, Phil decided to break the tension. 'This could be a coincidence. Nathan might still turn up alive and well.'

Andy nodded. 'Aye, I agree. But we can't ignore the similarities.'

'Do we have any pictures of the two men?' Alice suddenly asked.

'Jenny provided us with a recent shot of Nathan McLaren.' Dani glanced at Calder.

'I can get you plenty of photographs of Donald *and* newspaper cuttings about the disappearance. There should be stacks of information in the files too. They're all back home at my flat, but I can fetch them here by first thing tomorrow morning.'

'Good,' said the DCI. 'If Phil coordinates the CCTV trawl then I'd like Alice and Dan to make a trip back to Giffnock first thing. If Nathan still hasn't turned up by then we need to get proper statements from all the family members. You two might be able to develop a better relationship with Jenny McLaren. It seems Andy and I have got off to a bad start on that score.'

Chapter 6

Andy didn't really like returning to an empty flat. He knew Carol and Amy were enjoying themselves in Troon. He'd been receiving a constant barrage of text messages and photos. The weather was so good that they'd spent most of the time on the beach. Calder was forced to look at endless shots of his mother-in-law's ample form squeezed into a fancy bathing suit that looked like an exhibit from the Chelsea Flower Show. She was building sandcastles with Amy and beaming with pride.

He had to hand it to Carol's mum. She was great with kids. His own granny had barely laid down a fag for long enough to play with him or his sister. His Da's parents were long dead. Andy couldn't recall what they looked like at all.

Pouring a small whisky and setting the glass down on the coffee table, Andy looked closely at the photographs laid out before him. He'd dug out all the old boxes and albums he could find, selecting those shots which included his uncle.

There was one of Donald in his late teens, with Andy sitting on his lap. He must have been about four or five in this picture. To anyone coming across this snapshot, they'd assume the two boys were brothers.

His grandmother would have been a fair age when she had Donald – well into her forties. It was more common to be an older mum these days but would have been unusual back in the sixties. Andy wondered why there'd been such a big age gap between his father and Donald. He supposed it had simply happened that way. There were no IVF treatments in those days. You had a bairn whenever Nature decided it was acceptable.

Calder had a thought. Maybe there'd been miscarriages in between. The idea had honestly never occurred to him before. It wasn't something that was on his radar as a young lad. Only since Carol had begun looking into fertility treatments had he started considering these things properly. It wasn't a topic he would have dwelt on otherwise.

Andy glanced back at the photo. Don was wearing a pair of flared jeans and his dark hair was worn long and loose. Typical seventies get-up. Calder had adored his uncle. Don played the base guitar with a band for a while, when he was in his early twenties. Andy had thought he was a kind of Rock God. He couldn't have been more impressed if the guy was Jim Kerr himself.

Calder chuckled quietly, taking a slug of Scotch. Then he felt the tears prickling at his eyes. He saw the image of his Da's face before him, back when they were told that Don was missing. It was as if his bone structure had suddenly turned to jelly. Jack Calder was heartbroken. The jury was still out on whether Andy's father had ever properly recovered.

He wiped the dampness away from his cheeks with the back of his hand, sifting through more of the photographs and papers. Only the Calder family ever knew that Don had suffered from depression in the months leading up to his disappearance. They agreed at the time not to tell the investigating officer. Andy's uncle had never sought treatment for the condition, but his black moods were becoming more noticeable and frequent during the summer of 2005.

Mae remained adamant that her husband wouldn't have taken his own life. Andy's father was never so sure. Jack was certain that Don threw himself into White Cart Water, his body being swept into the wash of the Clyde and eventually out to sea.

But Mae insisted that the police should concentrate on finding Don alive, so she made the rest of the family swear they'd never speak of his battle with mental illness. Andy could see why she'd done it. The police may have stopped looking properly if they'd known, especially back then, when attitudes towards mental health problems were different than they were now.

Calder polished off the whisky and sat back against the sofa cushions, staring up at the ceiling, the heavy glass lying empty in his lap. This case in Giffnock changed everything. The circumstances were so similar it was startling. Andy had always believed in his heart that his Da was right. Uncle Don had topped himself, finally losing the battle with his inner demons. But now, his detective's instincts were going crazy. There had to be something else going on here. The thought of this possibility made his heart pound like a drum inside his chest.

*

When DCs Alice Mann and Dan Clifton returned to the McLarens' house in Giffnock, Jenny McLaren was much more subdued. Her sons sat on both sides of her at the solid wood dining table, making her appear small and fragile between their large, ungainly forms.

Ewan McLaren was a well-built lad of seventeen. He didn't hesitate to recount to the detectives every single detail of the day he'd spent with his father at the Glasgow Fair.

'Dad drove us to the station and we took the train into town.'

'Is your car missing too?' Dan Clifton interrupted, looking at the boy's mother.

She shook her head. 'The Audi is still in the garage and the Fiesta is sitting out on the driveway. But it looks as if Nathan took his house keys with him.' This thought made tears begin to pool in her eyes.

Clifton made a note in his pad. 'Okay. Carry on.'

'Cormac had arranged to meet his pals at the McLennan Arch at eleven. It was so busy there when we arrived that it took us about twenty minutes to find them. Cormac headed off into the park. We'd decided to keep in contact with each other on our mobile phones.'

'So *you* remained with your father for a while longer?' Alice clarified.

Ewan nodded. 'Aye, Dad and I had a bag of chips and wandered around the stalls for a while.'

'What was your father's mood like on Saturday? Was he enthusiastic about the trip?' Alice asked.

Ewan shrugged. 'We chatted and joked a bit. There were lots of groups about who looked as if they were on a mission to get pissed. Dad and I had a laugh about that.' He shot a cautious glance at his mother. 'It was a really hot day and there were plenty of lassies in shorts and bikini tops. Dad pointed a couple of the bonny ones out to me.'

Jenny visibly bristled.

'That was because he was trying to be pally, you know? Not because Dad is a sleazebag or anything.' Ewan gazed down at the table top. 'Then I bumped into a friend of mine and we left Dad by the river. It was near to where the university have their rowing club.'

'Aye, we know where that is,' Dan Clifton replied. 'Did your father say how he was going to spend the rest of the afternoon?'

Ewan looked up. His eyes were glistening. 'No and I never even bothered to ask.'

'I saw him later,' Cormac interrupted. 'We were on the dodgem's and Dad walked past. He waved at me and my pal, Billy. He looked like he was headed back towards the arch.'

'Going out of the park?' Alice stated.

'Aye, I suppose so,' he conceded.

'What time was this?'

'About 3pm maybe?'

'I didn't see Dad again until we met back at the station,' his older brother added. 'He called me on my mobile at about half five. I was ready to come home by then. It was a really hot day.' Ewan laid his palms out flat on the table. 'Dad had bought three burgers from a van and we ate them on the train. We chatted like normal and got home at seven.'

Dan looked at Jenny. 'Has there been any change in your husband's behaviour over the past few months? Any small alteration in his usual routines might give us an indication of what has happened to him.'

Jenny sighed. 'I've been thinking about nothing else these last twelve hours. I didn't pick up on anything different about Nathan at all. Everything's been normal.'

Ewan shifted about in his seat, as if he was suddenly uncomfortable.

'Have you got anything to add?' Alice asked him gently.

'I don't know if it's important.' His eyes flicked between the two people sitting beside him before resting on the female detective. 'Dad was talking to me a lot about the future. I suppose it's my age and everything – going off to uni and stuff. He was giving me advice about girls and finding my own way in life - the usual father-son spiel.'

'But they weren't the kind of topics your dad would normally discuss with you?'

'No, that's right. I got the feeling he was trying to tell me something. I don't know why, it was just a sense I had.'

Jenny swivelled her eyes in the direction of her eldest son. There was a puzzled expression on her face.

Alice Mann decided to leave the questions there. 'We will need to take a look around your house, Mrs McLaren, particularly in your husband's study. It would also be extremely useful to examine his computer back at the station.'

The woman rose up, her posture stooped. 'Of course, I'll show you where to go. His phone isn't there. I've been ringing it every half an hour since I realised he'd gone. But there's no reply.'

Alice nodded. She didn't tell the woman they'd already conducted a trace on Nathan McLaren's mobile phone number. They could pick up no signal at all from it. The device had either been disabled or destroyed. Instead, the detectives allowed Jenny to lead them solemnly out of the dining room, towards those parts of the house which had been her husband's domain.

Chapter 7

Carol Calder looked totally shattered. Her pretty face was sunburnt and a sprinkling of freckles had broken out across her cheeks. After throwing herself around the flat for an hour, Amy was finally fast asleep in her toddler bed.

Andy walked through to the lounge, where his wife was reclining, with her arms outstretched on the sofa. She was making no move to prepare them any dinner.

'Shall I fetch us a fish supper?' He asked tentatively, sensing Carol's mood may be volatile.

'Is that what you've been eating all weekend?' She shot back, with an accusatory glance at his broadening stomach.

Andy knew that Carol was simply exhausted. She'd have been up in the night with their daughter, what with her being in a strange bed and everything. He had the good sense not to rise to the bait. 'I ate at the cafeteria when I could. The menu is pretty healthy these days.'

Carol's expression softened. 'I'm sorry, sweetheart, I didn't mean to snap.' She put out her hand. Andy took it and sat on the sofa next to her, sliding his other hand over her curvy thighs, shown off rather nicely in a pair of tight fitting cotton Capri pants.

He nuzzled his face into her neck. 'I missed you.'

'Not enough to come along with us.'

Andy glanced up in alarm, but could see that she was still smiling. 'You know I had to work.'

Carol nodded, running her fingers through his thick hair. 'Was the Fair really busy? We watched the pictures on the news. It looked as if it was.'

'Aye, but it went off without any trouble.' He shifted himself up. 'But a man's gone missing from his home in Giffnock. He's 52 years old, married, with a couple of teenage kids. The circumstances are strikingly similar to what happened to Uncle Don.'

Carol's expression became serious. She and Andy hadn't been going out for long when Donald Calder had disappeared in 2005. The incident had threatened to end their budding relationship before it had even started. Andy became withdrawn and morose for several months afterwards. Carol felt a spasm of worry knot her stomach. The last thing she wanted was that sorry affair to be dragged up all over again. 'There can't be any connection, surely – not after all this time has passed?'

'I don't know. But we need to follow it up closely.' Andy clasped both her hands tightly. 'I might finally be able to find out what happened to him. Dad might get some answers at last.'

Carol forced a smile. 'Aye, perhaps.'

Andy leant forward and placed his lips over hers, feeling as if he could taste the salty spray of the sea coating Carol's soft skin. She kissed him back hard, running her hand underneath his shirt, lingering at the stubbly covering of hair that reached up to his belly button and tugging at his trousers, thinking that even though she was dog-tired she'd rather spend the evening making love than having to talk about the fate of Donald flaming Calder.

*

DCI Bevan squinted at the screen. 'Is it him?'

Phil shrugged his shoulders. 'I've looked through hours of tape. This was the only piece of footage where I thought I'd identified Nathan McLaren.' The

DS pointed at the grainy image of a man positioned right at the edge of the screen. 'That's the north bank of the river. It appears as if Nathan is speaking with one of the men at the rowing club. That group there have just come in off the water. Maybe Nathan knows him?'

Dani nodded. 'It's possible, yes. That's the University Boating Club, isn't it? Are all the members students?'

'I believe so, although I wasn't ever a rower myself,' Phil replied.

'Neither was I. My impression was that it was a pastime for the public school types.' The DCI contemplated this for a moment. 'I don't think it would be wise to send Andy down there. These people tend to wind him up. Could *you* get in touch with the club, and take Alice Mann there to conduct a few informal interviews?'

'Of course, Ma'am. I'll get onto it straight away.'

Bevan patted him lightly on the shoulder and returned to her office. Dani had other plans for Calder anyway. When she spotted Andy returning to his desk, she knocked on the window and beckoned him over.

The DC pushed open the flimsy door and peered around it. 'What's up, Ma'am?'

'Come in and take a seat.'

Andy raised his eyebrows and did what he was told. 'This sounds ominous.'

Dani leant forward, leaning her elbows on the desk. 'Not at all. I just want you to tell me all about Donald Patrick Calder.'

'It sounds like you already know some more about him.'

'I've had a read through the file, but I want your impressions.'

Andy sighed, balling his palms into fists in his

lap and then opening them out again, the suspect's way of playing for time. 'Don was your typical favourite uncle. He was a lot younger than my dad. He was funny, talented and enjoyed a bevvy.'

'I've looked at the photos. There's a strong family resemblance between the two of you.'

'I suppose I'm the age now that Don was when he went missing, give or take. But back in 2005 I was a fat bastard.' Andy laughed.

Dani didn't join in. She'd never have described her colleague in that way, even at the time when he'd suffered his heart attack two years ago. The DCI felt that her friend was far too harsh on his old self.

'The lassies always really went for Don, but he was devoted to Mae and the kids. He'd look at other women, sure, but that's as far as it ever went.'

'Did he discuss other women with you, down the pub, for instance?' Dani asked this casually, thinking she may have picked up on something here.

Andy shrugged. 'Not any particular lass.' He gave Dani a piercing look. 'You've got to understand, Ma'am. Men *do* talk about good looking women like that when they're all together in a group, even when they're married. It's just banter. It doesn't mean they're a womanizer.'

Dani nodded, making no comment. She wasn't entirely convinced that *all* men acted in this way. Alice Mann had recounted the interview she and Dan Clifton conducted with the McLarens. The DC mentioned that she thought the older son was hinting to them that his dad had an eye for the lassies. Bevan thought maybe Andy was doing the same. They both knew it might have a bearing on their disappearance, but neither wanted to sully their loved one's name.

'It *must* have been a theory that you and your parents considered – the possibility that Don had gone off with another woman?'

Andy sighed heavily. 'It was the possibility we *prayed* for. My dad was convinced that Don had killed himself. We would have been overjoyed if it turned out that the worst he'd done was run off with some tart and abandoned his wife and kids. But the years rolled past and we heard nothing. No letter or Christmas card. My dad and Uncle Donny had no family left in the world except each other, yet the man's no' been in touch for ten years. He's dead, Ma'am. There's no real question about that in my mind.'

'Then how did he wind up that way? You know as well as I do that men who die of unnatural causes have a weakness of some kind. It might be gambling, drugs or the lassies, but it's something that places them in harm's way.' Dani returned Andy's hard gaze.

Calder tipped his head back so that he was staring up at the ceiling. 'It was depression. Don had suffered from it on and off since he was a teenager.'

'There's nothing about it in the records.'

'Don had never gone for formal treatment. We didn't tell the investigating officer at the time he went missing.'

'Why on earth not?' Bevan was wide-eyed. 'You were surely not concerned about the stigma?'

Andy shook his head. 'Of course we weren't. Dad wanted to tell the police straight away. It was Mae who didn't want the issue raised. She didn't believe the depression had anything to do with Don going missing. Mae thought that if the police found out he had mental health problems, they'd write him off.'

Bevan thought that sadly there might have been some truth in that fear. 'Okay, well, we know about it now. Can I add this information to the file?'

Andy straightened himself up. 'Aye. It's important

that we find out the truth now. Attitudes on the force have changed a lot in the last ten years.'

Bevan was surprised by Calder's optimism. She sincerely hoped he was right.

Chapter 8

The park looked quite different to how it had at the weekend. The only folk to be seen now were the dog-walkers and the occasional jogger doing a circuit of the green. The grass was yellow and dry, despite the procession of sprinklers which were spinning water out onto its parched surface. DC Alice Mann noticed how these little fountains were creating a dozen mini rainbows in the strong morning sun.

Phil Boag had arranged a meeting with Anthony Lomond, the chief coach at the University Boating Club, down at their headquarters by the river. There was a training session currently in progress and Mr Lomond suggested this would provide a good opportunity to ask their questions.

A group of athletic-looking young men were hauling a boat up the jetty as they arrived. The sun was sparkling fiercely on the surface of the river, producing an almost blinding glare. Phil wished he'd brought his shades. An older man, although still no more than thirty, emerged from the wooden shed and approached the pair, putting out his hand and smiling broadly.

'You must be DS Boag. I'm Tony Lomond. You're in luck, the lads have just returned from a row. They'll be taking some refreshments before going out again.'

Tony led the police officers into the hut, which was pretty basic, but contained a kitchenette and a few tables and chairs. The walls were filled with framed photographs of sturdy young students holding aloft trophies. Lomond introduced them to the rowers, who were gathering in front of a serving hatch. He then led Phil and Alice towards one of the tables.

Phil brought out a photograph of Nathan McLaren. 'Do you recall having seen this man before?'

Lomond took the picture from him and examined it closely. 'Where might I have met him?' He eventually said.

'Nathan McLaren was seen talking to someone here at the boat sheds on Saturday, Mr Lomond. On the afternoon of the Glasgow Fair,' Alice explained.

He grimaced. 'There were hundreds of people milling about that day.' He looked at the face again. 'But I do believe I recognise him.'

'Do you mind if we show it around some of the lads?' Phil asked, 'whilst you consider where you might have seen this man before.'

'Of course, go ahead.'

Most of the rowers claimed never to have set eyes on McLaren. Then one young man paused for a moment, squinting hard at the image. 'This was on Saturday, you say?'

Phil nodded patiently.

'I couldn't swear to it, but I think this guy asked me about whether his son would be able to join the club, when he became an undergraduate at the university in September.'

Alice became immediately alert. 'What did you tell him?'

The boy scratched his head. 'I explained how I got involved in rowing and the kind of training we do, then I introduced him to Tony. I thought he'd know more about it than I would.'

Phil gestured for Lomond to come and join them. 'This lad says he directed Nathan McLaren to talk with you about his son maybe signing up to the rowing club. This was on Saturday afternoon.'

Tony's face seemed to light up with recognition. 'Ah, that was it. Nice chap. He'd done some rowing himself as a younger man. I gave him one of our leaflets and told him to encourage his lad to come along one Saturday morning for a trial. I'm always keen for enthusiastic new members to join, especially when the fourth years are about to graduate and move on.'

'Did he give you any indication of where he might be headed to after he spoke with you?'

'No, I'm afraid not. Look, something hasn't happened to the guy, has it? He seemed very pleasant.'

'He's gone missing. His family haven't set eyes on him since Saturday evening,' Phil replied flatly.

'Bloody hell,' Tony said with feeling. He watched silently as the pair of detectives left the hut, heading back across the arid green to their unmarked car, with a troubled expression on his face.

*

'We're beginning to create a timeline of sorts, for McLaren's movements on Saturday afternoon.' Dani pointed to her flip-chart. 'Ewan went off with his friend at around 1pm. We assume that Nathan remained within the park for the next couple of hours, being sighted talking with Tony Lomond at the rowing club at ten past three. According to Cormac's testimony, Nathan then left the park, exiting through the McLennan Arch, making his way into town. He met the boys again at Central Station at six, having bought some burgers from the van outside.'

'We haven't been able to get a sighting, either from witnesses or CCTV, of where he was in between,' Phil added.

'Have we had much response from the public?' Alice Mann asked.

'Nathan's disappearance hasn't had a great deal of publicity. It was mentioned briefly on the local news yesterday evening. The DCS is refusing to give me much of a budget on this. We're talking about a non-vulnerable, fifty-two year old miss-per who's only been gone a few days. He's not used his cash card since Saturday but he withdrew a couple of hundred then. McLaren could easily still be surviving on that money, wherever he is.'

Andy tutted loudly. 'Remember the amount of resources the division threw at the Maisie Riddell case? It's a bloody disgrace.'

'That was entirely different,' Phil responded swiftly, trying to keep his tone even. 'Maisie was only fourteen years old. She went missing from *school,* let's not forget.'

DS Boag was now in a relationship with Maisie's mother and his youngest daughter had been her best friend. Bevan hoped that Andy would be tactful and let the issue drop. It was clearly too close to home for Phil.

Calder grunted. 'I'm just sayin''

'The next course of action is to question his work colleagues. I'd like Alice and Dan to handle that please,' the DCI said quickly, keen to wind up the briefing before a row broke out. 'Andy, I'd like you to come along with me.'

'Sure thing, Ma'am. I'll just grab my jacket.'

Chapter 9

Jenny McLaren was perched on the edge of the sofa with her running gear on. Bevan noted how tanned and lean her legs were. 'Are you still in training for the marathon?' The DCI had endeavoured to keep the incredulity out of her voice but apparently failed.

'What the bloody hell else am I supposed to do? If I sit around this house waiting for news it'll drive me insane.'

'Have the boys gone to school?' Andy took the seat opposite her.

Jenny dropped her gaze and looked guiltily at the carpet. 'Ewan and his friend made up some missing person posters last night, with a photo of Nathan on. The boys have gone to stick them up around town - in the shop windows and on lamp posts. People have been very kind in their offers of help.' The woman lifted her head defiantly. 'You want to know why I'm not out there with them. Well, I'll tell you, shall I? I've not slept since Saturday night, so it's given me plenty of time to think. What I'm thinking is that Nathan has gone off someplace, with one of these *attractive women* he was encouraging *our* son to gawp at.'

There was a brief silence before Jenny crumpled. She slipped off the sofa onto the carpet and crawled into a ball, her entire body shaking with heaving sobs.

Dani got down onto her knees and placed her arms around the woman. 'Put the kettle on would you, Andy?'

Calder nodded and left the room.

'Do you really believe that Jenny?' She asked

gently, when the woman's crying had subsided.

'I know I'm not beautiful, DCI Bevan. But I'm slim and well-toned. I thought that was enough for Nathan. I've tried to keep myself healthy for him. I don't have the flab that other women of my age do. I wanted my husband to be proud of how I'd taken care of my body.' Her face sagged again, tears leaking from her small eyes.

'It may not be the case that your husband has absconded with another woman, Jenny. We found no suspicious messages on his e-mail or social media accounts. If he *had* left you for somebody else, he would very likely have informed you by now, or at least been in touch with one of the boys.'

Jenny lifted herself up into a sitting position, leaning her weight on one arm. 'What do you believe has happened then?'

Dani took a deep breath. 'Had you husband ever suffered from depression in the past?'

The woman's eyes widened in horror. 'You believe he's dead.' A hand flew up to cover her mouth, as if this idea hadn't occurred to her yet. Perhaps it really hadn't.

'Not necessarily, but we need to know everything about Nathan, so we can eliminate possibilities.'

Dani anticipated more hysteria but instead Jenny hoisted herself back into the seat. 'Nathan started going for therapy, a couple of years ago.'

Andy re-entered the room at this moment. He placed a tray of cups on the coffee table and sat back down in the armchair.

'We'd been having some, err... difficulties,' she stuttered.

Bevan remained crouched on the carpet in front of her. 'Of what kind, Mrs McLaren?'

'I didn't want to have sex any more. I just didn't enjoy it. Nathan was becoming frustrated with me.

He wanted us to seek outside help. In the end, I agreed to see the counsellor with him, but the exercises she suggested were just too excruciating for me to handle. I couldn't continue going.'

'But Nathan *did* continue to visit the therapist, without you present?'

Jenny nodded. 'He said he found it beneficial to talk things through. It wasn't a total disaster. Our sex life has been better since then. I realised how important it was to Nathan so I decided to provide him with what he wanted.'

Dani could sense Calder bristling in his seat behind her, even though the officer hadn't so much as moved a muscle during Jenny's speech. Bevan reached across for a mug of tea and handed it to their host. 'Here, have a sip of this.'

'So, I suppose you could say he'd been unhappy,' she continued. 'But things had got better in the last few months. I swear I hadn't seen anything like this coming.'

Dani rested her hand on Jenny's knee. 'I'm sure you didn't. But if you wouldn't mind, I'd like to take the contact details for the therapist your husband was seeing?'

The woman nodded sombrely, clasping the steaming mug with both hands, as if it wasn't hot at all. Bevan was seriously concerned she might scald herself so the detective prized the drink out of her vice-like grip, placing it carefully back on the table.

*

'Christ! No wonder the guy took off,' Andy declared, just as soon as Dani had closed the passenger door.

'Yes, it does sound as if their relationship was a little strained.'

'That's the understatement of the bloody century.

What did she say? "I decided I needed to give him what he wanted." The man must have felt like he was forcing himself on her, every single time they made love. Jeez, she's not exactly a looker to start with.' He visibly shuddered.

'Come on, Andy. Jenny McLaren is perfectly attractive. She's certainly very fit for her age.'

Andy shook his head. 'Oh, no, don't give me that one. Thin does *not* necessarily mean good-looking. That woman doesn't possess any of the attributes that real men find sexually appealing.'

Dani felt they'd stumbled into a discussion she didn't wish to pursue. 'Does it really matter, Andy? I'd rather not vilify the poor woman.'

'But it means that this case is totally different from what happened to Uncle Don, don't you see? Don was happily married to Mae, who was a real cracker. There's no way Donny left my aunt for another lassie.'

Dani shifted round in her seat. 'It doesn't work like that and you know it. Some of the world's most notorious philanderers had beautiful wives. It's about the excitement and the pursuit of a new experience. Whether or not a man will be unfaithful comes down to *his* character alone, not the attractiveness of his wife.'

Andy said nothing, he simply accelerated onto the motorway and gripped the steering wheel tightly, until his knuckles turned white.

As they approached the car-park of the Pitt Street Headquarters he finally said, 'is it okay if I drop you off here, Ma'am? I've got a couple of errands I need to run.'

'Of course.' Dani got out of the seat and closed the door. She stood and watched as Andy swept the car around and sped away from the entrance, his tyres screeching loudly in the process.

*

Andy knocked on the kitchen window. He could see Mae Mortimer pottering around inside. She jumped at the noise and put a hand up to her chest. Then her face broke into a smile when she saw who it was. Calder waited whilst she unlocked the French doors and pushed them open.

'Sorry to skulk about. I wasn't sure anyone was in, there wasn't a car out the front.' Andy stepped over the threshold, placing a kiss on his aunt's cheek.

'Mine is in the garage. Gavin is at work. I suppose it's hard for a policeman to shake off his habits. Your first instinct is to check round the back, isn't that right?' Mae gave a playful wink, padded over to a cordless kettle that looked as if it was quaintly old-fashioned but was clearly bang up-to-date and flicked it on.

Andy chuckled. 'Aye, and you wouldn't believe the kind of stuff we discover that way.'

'Oh, I think I can imagine. Now, to what do I owe this pleasure?' She folded her arms across her chest.

Andy ran a hand through his hair, leaving it standing up in little tufts. 'A man went missing, on Saturday night.'

Mae narrowed her eyes, blinking rapidly. 'What do you mean?'

Calder described the details of Nathan McLaren's disappearance. He tried to watch her reaction closely. But Mae turned swiftly to prepare the coffees and he couldn't see her face properly.

'Do you think there might be some kind of connection to Donny's case?' She stopped what she was doing, lowering her head.

Andy moved across the room and placed his hands on her shoulders. 'At first, I was shocked by the similarities. But now, I'm not so sure.'

Mae turned round, lifting her eyes to meet his. 'What do you think is different?'

'There were problems in this guy's marriage. The wife told us this morning. They'd stopped having sex months ago and were seeking counselling. It looks now as if Nathan has left of his own accord.' He cleared his throat. 'It made me wonder if you and uncle Don had been having any difficulties before he -,' Andy let his words trail away, seeing the dark shadow that passed across her face as he spoke them.

Mae took a step backwards and then slapped him hard on the cheek. 'How dare you come here and ask me that.'

Calder touched the hot skin, shocked by the severity of her reaction. 'I'm sorry. I should have used official channels. I put that far too bluntly.'

Abruptly, Mae seemed to realise what she'd done. Both hands flew up to cover her mouth. 'No, it's me who should apologise. I shouldn't have hit you, it's unforgivable.'

'I understand it's tough, with all these memories being brought back. I just thought this time around we might actually be able to get some answers.'

Mae lightly touched his stinging cheek with her fingertips. 'I'll need to put some ice on that. Otherwise they'll be a bruise.'

Andy caught her wrist, pulling her towards him. Mae shifted up so that she was sitting on the counter top, tipping her head back so that Andy could place his mouth over hers. They kissed urgently and Andy slipped his hand up her skirt. He pulled at her underwear, desperate to enter and possess the woman before him, as if this would heal the wound they both shared.

He pushed himself inside her and they moved

together in a steady rhythm, making no sound except the occasional gasp for breath. Then Andy cried out, as if he were in pain, withdrawing from her and turning away to secure his trousers, avoiding her gaze. 'Shit. I didn't realise I was going to do that. It really isn't why I came here.'

Mae put out her hand and brushed the palm against the tiny hairs on his neck. 'It just happened. Don't beat yourself up, Andy. It's because we both miss him so much.'

Calder twisted back and pulled her to him again, needing to feel her heart beating close to his chest. 'I know I should be feeling awful but I don't.' He whispered the words into her ear, nuzzling his face into her neck and gripping her tight, not ever wanting to let go.

Chapter 10

'It's just nostalgia, with a hint of mid-life crisis thrown in,' Phil said with a chuckle, pulling his chair up to the desk.

'What is?' Calder snapped, striding in at the tail end of the conversation.

Bevan turned towards him and smiled. 'Phil's going wild camping with some of his uni mates on Kintyre this weekend.'

Andy raised his eyebrows. 'Not planning on breaking the law I hope DS Boag. Be careful, or you'll wake up to find DCI Bevan shining a torch in your face at 2am.'

Dani laughed.

'We've checked out the legislation very carefully, as it happens. There are several landowners who are happy to open up their fields for public use.'

Calder placed his hands in the air. 'Fine by me. What you get up to during the weekends is your own business. Live and let live is my motto.'

Boag grinned. 'Alice has supplied me with the transcript of her interviews with McLaren's workmates, Ma'am.'

'Anything of interest in there?' Bevan enquired.

'Nathan was generally acknowledged to be a quiet and capable work colleague. His boss rated him very highly. Apparently, he was one of the best financial systems analysts in the business.'

'Whatever the hell that means,' Andy chipped in dryly.

Dani wondered what was eating him, but concentrated on Phil's briefing instead. 'Is there anyone at the office who McLaren confided in – a pal he went for drinks with, perhaps?'

'One of the female employees seemed to know him quite well.' Phil scanned the sheet. 'Mhairi Henderson.' The DS spotted Alice Mann by the coffee machine and called her over. 'What did Miss Henderson tell you about Nathan?'

Alice addressed the DCI. 'Mhairi is on Nathan's project team, they've got to know one another very well over the past few years. She didn't have any idea of where he might have gone, but she was certainly aware that Nathan and his wife hadn't been getting along for a while.'

'Could this woman be the girlfriend?' Andy asked.

Alice shook her light brown bob. 'No, Mhairi is only in her late twenties and she's really quite overweight. My feeling was that she was a non-threatening confidante for McLaren. If you saw her, you'd know what I meant.' The DC shifted from one foot to the other, looking awkward, as if she'd broken an unspoken rule of political correctness.

But Calder nodded assuredly, indicating he understood perfectly well. 'This lassie could be very useful to us then.'

'Yes,' Dani agreed. 'It might be worth speaking to her again outside the office environment. Did you build up any kind of rapport with her?'

Alice made a face. 'It was Dan who Mhairi seemed to open up to. I reckon she thought he was cute.'

'Good, then I'll send DC Clifton to talk with Miss Henderson again. You can tag along too, Alice, so she doesn't feel nervous being alone with him. We want her comfortable and relaxed. That way she might let something slip.'

Alice nodded. 'Right you are, Ma'am.'

DCI Bevan's mobile began ringing insistently. She answered it and listened in silence, ending the call politely. 'That was Jenny McLaren. She believes that her sons' posters may have elicited some fresh information.' Dani turned towards Calder. 'Come on, let's go and check it out.'

*

Cormac and Ewan were both at home with their mother. It was the McLaren's eldest son who took charge when the officers arrived.

'A lady came to our door this morning. She'd seen the poster we put up in the window of the Quick Stop Shop on the High Street,' he explained breathlessly.

'Do you have the name and address of this woman?' Bevan immediately asked.

'Yes, I've written it all down,' Jenny added, handing over a sheet of paper, ripped from a memo pad.

'What did she say?'

'She recognised the picture of Dad,' Ewan continued, jittery with excitement. 'The woman was walking her dog in Balgray Park late on Saturday evening – just before ten, she thinks. According to her, Dad passed her on the path that runs beside the reservoir.'

'Was he alone?'

Ewan nodded. 'Yes, she said he was.'

Bevan and Calder exchanged glances.

'Did Nathan go to Balgray often? Did he jog there, or fish perhaps?' Dani directed this question to Jenny.

'No, we've been to the country park from time to time for a stroll, but it certainly wasn't somewhere we went to regularly.' The woman looked bemused. 'How did he get to the reservoir without the car?'

'That's a question that we'll have to look into,' Dani said gently. 'First, we will need to speak with this witness ourselves.'

The DCI promised to inform the family of any progress on the lead as soon as they were able. Then she ushered Calder out of the house, intending to return to headquarters as swiftly as possible.

*

The air was warm, but there was a strong breeze blowing across the reservoir, making the grey water lap up at the artificial shoreline. Dani felt the landscape was bleak and unappealing.

After gaining a formal statement from Mrs Kathleen York of Duncan Terrace, Barrhead, the DCS agreed to provide Bevan with a search team. The uniformed men and women were stretching out in a semi-circle across the scrubland, sniffer dogs straining at their leashes just a few strides ahead.

Dani scanned the area with her binoculars.

'It's a perfect place to dump a body,' Andy commented evenly.

'Aye, it's the first thing that crossed my mind when Ewan mentioned the location. But there's a seven mile network of paths here and the only witnesses to what goes on in much of it are the wildlife.'

'Nathan must have got here by car at that time in the evening. There would have been very few buses still running,' Calder went on. 'Which means that someone else brought him, or he took a taxi cab. My guess is that he didn't stray more than a mile and a half from the Balgraystone Road car park.'

'Which just leaves the area around the reservoir itself.' Dani gazed back out at the rippling waves. 'Nathan may have jumped off the railway bridge into the water. He would have been heading in that general direction from the spot where Mrs York saw him. It was becoming dark by ten. It would have been difficult for anyone to have observed him go in.'

The pair of detectives walked along the path which circumnavigated the reservoir. As they drew closer to the brick built bridge which carried the Neilston Railway line over the water, DCI Bevan gestured for one of the search team to follow them. The nearer they got, Bevan noticed the officer having increasing trouble keeping the German Shepherd on its lead.

'Can he sniff out a cadaver even if it's in the water?' Dani called across to the man.

'Oh, aye, as long as it's near enough to the surface.'

'Let him go, then.'

The sleek animal immediately streaked across the shrubland to the water's edge. The dog poked its nose around the base of one of the bridge's supports. Bevan and Calder trotted over to see what he'd found.

The uniformed officer knelt down and patted the dog on its head. 'Good boy, what have you got for us, eh?'

Andy stepped gingerly down the bank, resting his hand against the mossy brickwork for support. The dog was nuzzling a black bin bag which was caught in the circling current between the vegetation and the bridge. The two men hauled it up out of the water.

Dani could recognise the smell from several feet away. 'I'll call out the white coats,' she shouted over. 'Just leave it there for now. We'll set to work getting a cordon rigged up.'

Chapter 11

'Well, it certainly wasn't suicide,' Andy stated sagely, as they supped their pints in the newly refurbished pub across the road from headquarters.

'We won't get the PM results back until tomorrow.' Dani lifted her glass of white wine and took a mouthful.

'But we're sure it's Nathan McLaren?' Phil enquired.

'Yup,' Andy supplied. 'His face was badly bloated and there was some decomposition evident, but it was obviously him.'

'I'm not going to inform the family officially until I've got confirmation from the pathologist. I've told Jenny we've found a body, of course, and that she should prepare herself for the worst.'

'The McLarens are going to have a bloody awful night then.' Phil whistled through his teeth.

'Yes,' Dani said carefully, placing her glass down on the table. 'But it would be far worse for her to have seen him in that condition. The corpse looked grotesque. He'd obviously been in the water since Saturday night. I'm not an expert, but from what we saw, the man had been badly beaten about the face and torso.'

'At least we'll get a decent budget from the DCS now.' Andy polished off his pint.

Dani shot him a disapproving glance.

'I only meant that it will become a full-blown murder investigation and not remain a missing persons' case that gets forgotten in a few weeks.'

'We'll need to get the names of every jogger, dog-walker, courting couple and flasher who was roaming around the Balgray Country Park on Saturday evening. Christ, it'll be one hell of a job.'

'The question is – did he meet his murderer there, or did this person drive Nathan McLaren to Balgray?' Phil looked at each of his colleagues in turn.

'I doubt the car park's got CCTV,' Andy chipped in. 'It's just a gravelled area scooped out of the scrubland.'

Phil rose from his stool. 'Another?'

Unexpectedly, Andy shook his head. 'No thanks, Pal. I need to head off.'

'Thanks for the offer, Phil, but I'll have to be making tracks myself, tomorrow is going to be a tough day.' Dani turned to Calder. 'Can you give me a lift? I've put my wee car into the shop.'

Andy shifted awkwardly in his seat. 'Actually, I've got an errand to run on the way home, I really can't.'

Dani couldn't hide her surprise. She'd banked on Calder going her way. He always had to get straight home for Carol and Amy. It hadn't crossed her mind she'd end up stranded.

'If no one's staying for another bevvy then I'll drive you, Ma'am,' Phil said matter-of-factly.

'But it's out of your way,' Dani argued.

'The girls are with Jane tonight. It's really not a problem.'

Bevan thought she noticed Andy's cheeks redden, although she quickly dismissed this idea. He wasn't the type.

'I'll see you bright and early,' he muttered, grabbing his jacket and swiftly exiting the pub.

Phil raised his eyebrows as Calder allowed the glass panelled door to bang shut behind him. 'I wonder where he's off to in such a hurry.'

'Aye,' said Dani, swigging back the final dregs of wine. 'Where indeed.'

Bevan noticed that her team had a different air about them today. The fact this was now a murder inquiry had made her officers more alert, she could already sense the tension in the room.

'I want Dan and Alice to question Mhairi Henderson again today. Wait until she's home from work. Once she knows that Nathan is dead, the girl may open up a bit more,' the DCI announced.

'What does the pathologist's report tell us?' Andy asked Bevan directly.

Dani slipped a pile of photographs out of an envelope and began attaching them to the boards. 'Nathan McLaren died some time on Saturday night. The pathologist can't be any more precise than that. It's been very warm since then and inside that black bag it became incredibly hot, even if the water brought the temperature down a little.'

DC Clifton grimaced, observing the gruesome effect the heat had had on the corpse.

The DCI continued, 'Nathan's body had been viciously beaten before death. But Dr Muir found fragments of material in his mouth and throat. This discovery, in addition to the blueness of the face, made the pathologist conclude that Nathan had died of asphyxiation.'

'Was there any indication of what had been placed in his mouth?' Phil enquired.

Dani shook her head. 'There was nothing in the bin bag or near the dump site. We have to assume the killer took it with them. Dr Muir suggested a scarf of some kind, or a small item of clothing, like underpants or a sock.' She took a deliberate step forward. 'Dr Muir discovered something else. While they were stripping the body, he was surprised to note that the wedding ring was missing from his left hand.'

'It's not so surprising, if Nathan was planning to meet a lover,' Phil declared. 'He'd probably taken it off.'

Dani raised an eyebrow. 'Aye, but the doc didn't find it in his pocket. The ring was only discovered well into the PM. It was stuck halfway along Nathan McLaren's oesophagus.'

'Is that what killed him?' Phil's face had gone white.

'Dr Muir believes that Nathan would still have been able to breathe with the obstruction there. It was whatever was stuffed in his mouth later that suffocated him.'

'So, this killing might not have been premeditated,' Andy suggested. 'If the murderer's only weapon was fists plus whatever came to hand to smother the victim.'

'It's possible. But there's another aspect too.' Dani shifted her weight from one foot to the other. 'Dr Muir found evidence of recent sexual activity on the body. He believes that McLaren was subject to anal penetration at some time before his death.'

'Rape?' Alice Mann asked.

Bevan shrugged her shoulders. 'It's inconclusive. There were physical signs of sex but no semen deposits. The perpetrator either used a condom or a foreign body to penetrate McLaren.'

Andy Calder's face had lost its colour. 'Was McLaren a homosexual? Is that what he was doing in that park – cruising for a bloke?'

'I think we have to assume that's the case. Unless somebody here believes there's another, more plausible explanation for Nathan McLaren's presence in Balgray Park at 10pm on a Saturday night?'

Bevan glanced around at the officers standing

before her. Nobody uttered a single word.

Chapter 12

Mhairi Henderson lived with her parents in a detached house in Pollok. The young woman had not been home long from work when DCs Clifton and Mann turned up.

Mhairi seemed surprised to see the police officers again. Mrs Henderson offered to make them all tea and Alice Mann agreed, thinking the girl might need it after they delivered the bad news.

They sat in a large conservatory, which was semi-circular in shape and provided an impressive view out towards Crookston Castle. Mhairi had dyed her hair jet-black and her make-up was deliberately applied in order to accentuate dark, almond shaped eyes. She wore a piercing through her nose and was a least a couple of stone overweight. Her mother returned with the drinks and a plate piled high with cakes and biscuits. The fiercely independent Alice felt that Mhairi might do well to move out of home and into her own place, where she could regulate her lifestyle better.

Dan shifted forward in his seat. 'I'm afraid we have distressing news, Mhairi. Nathan McLaren is dead. His body was found yesterday.'

The girl put a chubby hand up to her crimson mouth. Tears began to streak down her face. 'What happened to him? Was there an accident?'

'No,' Dan continued gently. 'We believe he was murdered.'

Mhairi's eyes widened. 'Who would want to murder Nathan?'

'Miss Henderson, you told us before that Nathan was having some problems with his wife. Did he give any indication of what might have caused these difficulties?'

She looked uncomfortable. 'I only knew about it because of working right next to him. Their phone conversations were really tense. One day, Nathan actually made a joke out of it. I suppose he needed to let off steam. After that, he would tell me the odd detail about what went on at home. I think he liked to have someone to confide in.'

'Did you ever meet Jenny McLaren?'

'Yes, a few times at work dos. She looked at me as if I was something that had just crawled out from under a stone.' Mhairi said this without self-pity. 'You know, the way that really thin and fit people do when faced with someone like me. My existence seems to actually disgust them.'

'So you didn't like Mrs McLaren very much?'

'Have you met her? She's horrible.' Mhairi lifted her mug and took a tentative sip. 'I don't know why Nathan stayed with her. For the boys I suppose. They are both really nice.' She sighed. 'Poor things, they'll be stuck with her now.'

'Was there anything else that Nathan confided in you about? Did he have feelings for anyone other than his wife, for example?' Dan opened his hands out with their palms facing upwards, trying to project an image of being as open and friendly as possible.

Mhairi's eyes began to search around the room for something other than the detectives to settle on. 'I dunno, not really.'

'This is important,' Alice chipped in. 'Nathan is dead now and we need to find his killer, to stop anyone else suffering the same fate. He wouldn't want this person to get away with it. I'm sure Nathan would rather his secrets got out than a murderer went free.'

Mhairi's eyes shot back to the DC. This point appeared to have hit home. 'Nathan never actually told me, but I knew. I had loads of gay friends at college.' She laughed bitterly. 'Gay men like me much better than straight ones. I think Nathan quite fancied one of the guys in our office. He's a real hottie. We used to smirk at one another when he came near our desk and bent down to get stuff out of a drawer. I know it sounds bad, but it was like a release for Nathan – to be able to laugh about his feelings with someone else and not be condemned for it. I would *never* have told his wife. I'm not happy about telling you now, but you're right. Nathan wouldn't want a murderer to be loose out there because of *his* secret. He'd want to protect other men.'

'Would you be prepared to make a formal statement about this?'

She nodded. 'Aye, as long as I don't have to face Jenny McLaren, I would.'

*

DCI Bevan had left it for as long as she could before speaking with Jenny McLaren. Unfortunately, the woman insisted on seeing her husband's body. A car was sent out to Giffnock to pick her up and ferry her to the headquarters. Bevan suggested that she bring a friend or relative with her, but not one of the boys.

Jenny was accompanied by a lady who looked to be a good decade older. She introduced herself as Helen, a neighbour of the McLarens.

Dani took Jenny's arm and led her into a small room, where she could observe Nathan's body through a glass screen. The pathologist had done the best job he could. The head had been carefully positioned so that only one side was visible.

Mrs McLaren gasped when she saw him. 'Why is his skin that colour?'

'Your husband was in the water for several days.'

'Is that what happens then – when a body's been dead for a while?'

Dani laid a hand on her arm. 'Yes. Would you like to be left alone?'

Jenny shook her head. 'I don't want to remember him like that.'

The DCI led her out. They headed towards the relatives' room. Alice had been instructed to take the neighbour elsewhere for a coffee. Dani helped Jenny into a seat.

'I need to ask you some more questions.'

Jenny looked up, her expression blank. 'What about?'

Normally, Dani would have held the woman's hand at this point, but in this instance, she didn't feel it would help. 'As a result of our inquiries, we have reason to suspect that your husband was meeting someone in Balgray Park on the evening he was killed.'

'Who was he meeting – what for?'

Dani wasn't sure if the woman was being deliberately bloody-minded. She cleared her throat. 'I've spoken with Nathan's therapist, who confirmed that your husband had been battling with his homosexual urges for quite some time.'

Jenny's bottom lip wobbled. 'You think he was meeting up with a man.'

'Had it happened before?'

'I don't know.' She hugged her thin arms around that bony frame. 'I found a magazine that was full of pictures of men, you know, in compromising positions. This was about six months ago. It was in his briefcase. I confronted him about it. That was around the time that I stopped sleeping with him. I was humiliated. It felt as if he was thinking about those disgusting men I'd seen in the magazine whilst he was making love to me. I couldn't bear it. Eventually, I agreed to go to the counsellor with him. But for the first couple of sessions it seemed like the process was all for his benefit. The therapist was full of sympathy for Nathan and how he'd had to suppress his true desires for all these years. It was as if our twenty years of marriage meant nothing.'

'So you stopped attending the sessions and Nathan carried on alone.'

Jenny clasped her hands together, absent-mindedly twisting her wedding ring. This action reminded Dani of what had happened to her husband's. 'I believe that Nathan had already made his mind up about the future. Now I'd found out the truth he could finally live the life he'd always wanted.' She looked up, her eyes full of pain. 'Where did that leave me and the boys?'

'You should have told us this when Nathan first went missing,' Dani said quietly.

She sighed in frustration. 'Nathan was still the same man. I never thought for a moment that he would go out in the middle of the night to have sex in a *public park*. There was nothing *to* tell.'

Dani could appreciate her point. She left the room to fetch the neighbour to take her home. There was nothing to be gained now by haranguing the poor woman.

Chapter 13

Andy Calder was in a bad mood. Dani had noted this as soon as he entered her office alongside his colleagues. There was something about the way he plonked himself down on the sofa, keeping his shoulders hunched, which gave it away to his boss.

'Now the press have got onto it, DCS Nicholson is breathing down my neck for a quick result,' she began. 'Where are we with the appeal for witnesses?'

Alice Mann flipped open her notebook. 'We've had a slow trickle of phone calls from folk who were in Balgray Park on Saturday evening. But no one appears to have seen anything suspicious.'

'Is the area known for being a cruising point? Do homosexuals and courting couples use the car parks at night?' Dani glanced at each officer in turn.

'Not that I could tell,' Phil chipped in. 'I've been in contact with some of the gay pressure groups in Glasgow since we discovered why Nathan McLaren was in Balgray Park when he was killed. The guys there said it wasn't a well-known meeting place, but then, they also said that cottaging is generally less common these days. Homosexuality doesn't have the stigma it once did.'

'It still does if you're a gay bloke married to a woman,' Dan Clifton added.

'Aye.' Bevan nodded. 'Bloody good point. So, this man we're looking for – was he Nathan's boyfriend, or just a casual pick-up? I think that's the key to this investigation.'

'There was absolutely nothing out of the ordinary on Nathan's computer,' Alice responded. 'No deleted messages from a male lover or evidence of gay porn.'

'Jenny claimed that Nathan had some porn mags in his briefcase. Perhaps he and his lover kept it old-fashioned and corresponded by letter?'

'We found nothing in his office, either at home or at work, Ma'am,' Dan confirmed.

'My sense is that Nathan was only just beginning to act upon his urges,' Bevan continued. 'His wife had only known about his proclivities for a few months. The therapist was encouraging him to explore them further. If there was a boyfriend, I suspect he was fairly new on the scene.'

'I reckon that would make Nathan vulnerable,' Phil said carefully. 'He was almost like a teenager taking their first, tentative steps onto the dating circuit. He might have appeared pretty green to those who'd been out for many years.'

'And a bit naïve perhaps,' Alice added, crinkling her forehead. 'I think we should go back to that rowing club, Ma'am. I've got a hunch that McLaren wasn't simply hanging around there to find out whether his son could join in September. I believe there's something else.'

Bevan narrowed her eyes thoughtfully. 'Okay. You and Dan make another trip over there. Talk to some more people this time and have a proper conversation with that coach.'

Alice nodded, recognising the DCI's tone as an indication they were dismissed. As the officers filed out of the poky room, Dani gestured for Calder to remain seated. She pulled the door shut behind Phil.

'You were very quiet during the briefing,' Bevan stated, crossing her arms over her chest.

'I know what you're thinking.'

Dani cocked her head to one side and raised an eyebrow.

'You think that Uncle Donny might have been

meeting a fella too, on the night he went missing.' Andy kept his gaze fixed on the floor. 'Donny was *not* a homosexual,' he seethed through gritted teeth. 'I want to make that absolutely clear, Ma'am.'

Dani took a deep breath. 'If the McLaren case is going to prove difficult for you to work on, then I'll have to re-assign you. There's no place for prejudice on my team, or for anyone who can't keep an open mind. If you are too close to this, I'll find something else for you to do.'

He glanced up in surprise. 'I want to remain on the investigation. This is really important to me.'

'Okay, Andy, but I need you to keep focussed on Nathan McLaren. You've been distant and distracted these last few days. It's time to step up now. There's a killer out there, who we've got to catch.'

He nodded. 'Aye, of course. I'm a hundred percent committed to this case, I swear.'

*

Mae slid her hand across Andy's torso, pulling him closer. 'I saw on the news that they'd found that man's body.'

Calder's muscles tightened. 'I can't discuss the details.'

She shifted up, resting her chin on his chest. 'I know he was dumped in Balgray Reservoir. The reporter said so.' Mae widened her green eyes and looked straight at him. 'I want them to send divers down – to see if Don's body is in there too.'

Shocked by her words, Andy sat bolt upright. 'I don't believe the McLaren case has *anything* to do with Don's disappearance now. There are too many differences. Balgray is a good five miles from here. What would Uncle Don be doing all the way over in Barrhead that night?'

'Well, what was Nathan McLaren doing there?'

Andy remained silent, certainly not wishing to get into that territory.

'Exactly, who knows why his killer took him there. Because it was quiet, I suppose, and the reservoir was the perfect place to dump a body,' Mae continued.

Calder could tell she'd spent a while considering this.

'If the same man murdered Don all those years ago then he could be in that place as well. Surely the police can at least search for him? You must be able to request it?'

Calder gazed at her beautiful, anguished face and groaned. He leaned in and kissed her forehead tenderly. 'He isn't there. You have to trust me on this, sweetheart. The McLaren murder has nothing to do with Don. I know more of the details than you do. I promise it's a dead end.'

Mae's lips began to quiver. Tears spilled down her cheeks. Andy kissed them away but they continued to fall. 'I need to know what happened,' she sobbed. 'I thought I was finally going to find out where he was, so we could bury him.'

'I know,' Calder whispered, holding her close, smoothing her soft hair. 'We *will* find out the truth about what happened to Donny, I swear to you. But just not this time.'

Chapter 14

DCs Mann and Clifton arrived at the Clydebank University Campus by mid-morning. Both young detectives were graduates themselves and familiar with the environment. There were very few students in residence on the site at this time of the year but they had arranged to meet Tony Lomond at the cafeteria by the entrance to the Department of Environmental Planning, where he was a post graduate student.

The building was modern, allowing the bright sunlight to stream onto the tables through tall strips of glass reaching up to a high ceiling. Lomond was looking smart in an open-necked blue striped shirt. He already had a coffee in front of him when the two officers arrived.

'How much longer do you have until you graduate?' Alice asked with genuine interest, thinking that the man must be thirty at least.

'There's another year remaining on my Msc course. But I'm preparing to produce a doctoral thesis, that's why I'm here working through the holidays. I'm already teaching classes, but would like to go for a permanent tenure once I have my Phd.' He sipped his espresso. 'I don't really understand why you're speaking to me again. I've nothing more to add.'

'Did you happen to see on the news that Mr McLaren's body was found in Balgray Reservoir yesterday?'

Tony adopted a grave expression. 'Yes, I did. It's terribly sad for the man's family. He seemed like such a pleasant chap.'

'This is now a murder inquiry,' Dan explained reasonably. 'You are one of the last people to speak with Nathan McLaren before his death. Could you do your very best to recall exactly what the man said to you and which direction he headed in after he left the Rowing Club on Saturday afternoon?'

Tony narrowed his grey eyes, as if in deep concentration. 'As I said, he explained how he rowed himself whilst he was studying at St Andrews. I believe he told me that he was now a business software analyst, his office was somewhere in town.' The man paused, blinking several times before adding, 'he may have mentioned that he was going to visit a bar in the city centre, before meeting his sons later.'

'You didn't say this when we spoke to you earlier.' Alice fixed upon him a stern stare. 'Did he give you the name of the bar?'

Tony cleared his throat, obviously growing uncomfortable. 'I think it was called Bacchus.'

'The gay bar?' Clifton enquired.

Tony sighed heavily. 'Look, my sexuality is a private matter. I teach here and train the lads down at the river without any problems whatsoever. They don't need to know what I do in the evenings and at weekends. My parents don't know about my lifestyle either and I really don't believe it's anyone else's business.'

'Were you sleeping with Nathan McLaren?' Alice interrupted bluntly.

Lomond's cheeks flushed pink. 'Why, do you have sex with every straight man you come into contact with?' He immediately put his hands up in the air. 'I'm sorry, that was out of line. But no, in answer to your question, I had not ever slept with Nathan McLaren. I'd seen him a few times at clubs and bars in town, that's all. When he was wandering around the Green on Saturday, he saw us practising and came over. Nathan was genuinely interested in his son joining up, but then he recognised me.'

'That must have been extremely awkward for you, sir,' Dan said evenly.

'It wasn't ideal, sure, but Nathan and I had a brief, private conversation and then he headed off. The guy had absolutely no interest in outing me in front of my friends any more than he would wish to be outed himself. I'd say that Nathan had a lot more to lose on that score than I did.'

'Actually, Mrs McLaren had been aware of her husband's sexuality for several months,' Alice corrected.

'But I'm sure she didn't know he was frequenting gay bars during his lunch hour, the ones best known as pick-up joints.' Tony polished off his coffee, seeming frustrated by their line of questioning.

'Could you supply us with a list of these places, Mr Lomond? And if you can recall the dates that you saw Nathan in these bars it would be extremely helpful. We will also have to ask you not to leave the city for the foreseeable future, not until our investigation is completed.'

Tony said nothing, but nodded his head in silent resignation.

*

Although it was only late morning, Bacchus was already busy with lunchtime drinkers. The clientele were predominantly male, most wearing tight fitting business suits, looking well-groomed and professional.

Alice noticed that Dan was getting some appraising glances as they approached the bar. She had to admit that her partner was quite cute, in a floppy-haired, boyish kind of way. Alice asked the barman if they could talk to the manager. The detective was surprised to see it was a woman, although she wasn't sure why that should be unusual.

Tanya Smith looked closely at the photograph DC Clifton handed her. 'Aye, he was in fairly often, usually at lunchtimes during the week.'

'Did this man drink here on his own, or with others?' Alice had to raise her voice above the pounding beat of the music.

'He always comes in on his own, but he chats to folk, including the bar staff. I'd say he's friendly rather than a shark – you know, someone here just to pick-up. I got the sense he was lonely, maybe. The guy *is* a little older than our usual customers.'

'Was he in on Saturday afternoon?'

Tanya made a face. 'We were incredibly busy on Saturday. There were lots of people here from out of town. Plenty who most likely didn't know this is a gay bar, which doesn't matter in the slightest. Everyone is welcome. If that chap was in, there's absolutely no chance I'd remember, sorry.'

'Have you got CCTV cameras?'

'Only at the front and back, not here in the bar area. We very rarely have any trouble at Bacchus. Our clientele are regulars and we're like a family.'

'Do you mind if we talk to some of your customers?'

Tanya adopted a hostile stance. 'Actually, I'd rather you didn't. I like to run a relaxed and tolerant operation here. The people who drink at Bacchus don't expect to have their lifestyle questioned.'

Alice held the photograph up again, tapping her finger on the grainy image. 'The man who you recognised was called Nathan McLaren. He was brutally murdered on Saturday night. I'm sure your customers would be very happy to assist us in finding out who was responsible.'

Tanya looked genuinely shocked. 'Shit, he was that fella on the news. I never made the connection – he was married with kids they said...' realisation seemed to dawn on the manageress. 'Okay, fine, ask ahead, just try to tread gently. Remember, it's not a crime any longer to practise an unconventional lifestyle.'

Alice felt that Ms Smith was preaching to the converted with this warning but that she could certainly think of a good number of her colleagues who would be only too pleased to see homosexuality made illegal again. Nodding their thanks, the DC flipped open her notepad, nudging her partner to do the same and began circulating the room.

Chapter 15

'All of our interviews suggest that Nathan was a pleasant, quiet guy, new to the scene. He was getting to know people rather than cruising.' Alice Mann addressed her colleagues. 'We took some names and addresses, but none of these men knew McLaren particularly well, or so they claim. I think that Tony Lomond is the only one who we should consider a proper suspect.'

Phil Boag stepped forward. 'The Barrhead station had a call from a local cabbie. He recalls taking a man of Nathan McLaren's description to the car-park by the reservoir at roughly 9.30pm on Saturday night. He picked him up from the end of the High Street in Giffnock. McLaren didn't ask him to stay and wait.'

'McLaren could have been meeting Lomond there. Both men would have been approaching from different directions. They wouldn't necessarily have travelled to Balgray Park together.' Alice felt excited by this piece of evidence. 'Maybe Lomond's flat was too far for Nathan to get to late in the evening, so they chose neutral territory somewhere between their two places.'

'What is Lomond like – would he be physically capable of over-powering McLaren?' Dani looked at both of the DCs.

Clifton nodded. 'Definitely, Ma'am. Lomond is twenty years younger and a rower. He's got impressive upper body strength.'

'Then I suggest that we ask Tony Lomond to come in to the station voluntarily to provide us with a statement. I want to know exactly what he was doing on Saturday night after 9pm.'

'But what would his motive be?' Andy Calder chipped in. 'Nathan was unlikely to reveal Tony's sexuality to the university. McLaren wasn't exactly out and proud himself.'

'Perhaps there was an argument between the two men,' Alice offered. 'One of them wanted to take things further and the other didn't. My guess would be that Nathan McLaren became too attached to Lomond. Potentially, this was Nathan's first ever relationship with a man, he could have been overwhelmed by the feelings he had.'

Dani nodded. 'It's certainly plausible, but at the moment it's just supposition. We can't make Lomond our prime suspect purely because he is a gay man who happened to pass the time of day with Nathan on the afternoon before he was killed. We've got to do far better than that.'

'Our victim could have visited any number of bars in the city centre in the hours leading up to his murder,' Phil asserted. 'Glasgow was heaving with people. He could have arranged to meet any one of them later that evening at the park.' The DS glanced at his boss. 'I think we should get an outside advisor in, Ma'am.'

'How do you mean?'

'I took a look at the criminal profiler list this morning. There's a new name on it. Professor Rhodri Morgan from the University of Glasgow; in his biog, it states he wrote the best-selling true-crime book about Ian Cummings.'

'The man who murdered all those young men down in London in the late eighties?'

Phil nodded. 'Yep. Cummings had targeted the homosexual community in west London. He's now serving a life sentence in Broadmoor. There was a campaign about twelve years back to get him released. That was when Professor Morgan wrote the book. He argues in it that Cummings should never be let out, that he lacks any real understanding of the impact of his crimes.'

'You seem to know a lot about it,' Andy said with a grin.

'Well, I've read the professor's book, it's very good.' Phil cleared his throat. 'My brother was living in London at the time the murders took place. Colin is gay and settled down south with his partner. We were very worried about him at the time these killings were taking place. My parents wanted Colin to move back to Scotland. It was a great relief to my family when Cummings was caught. I've had an interest in the case ever since.'

Calder looked embarrassed.

'I think it's a great idea, Phil,' Dani responded. 'Can you get in contact with Professor Morgan and set us up a meeting? I think it would be worth shelling out some of our budget on this. For the time being, let's get what we can out of Tony Lomond. Then we can at least strike him off the suspect list.'

*

Dani put down the phone after an awkward conversation with her boyfriend. She wouldn't be able to spend the weekend with him in Edinburgh now, not with the McLaren case going on. James seemed to understand and was very sweet about it, but Dani wondered if he really knew what being in a relationship with a copper was like. Not just at the beginning, but months and years in, when there had been many such let downs and disappointments. Bevan shook this thought from her mind, padding into the kitchen of her ground floor flat to fix a glass of whisky.

She sipped it standing by the patio doors, staring out into the tiny garden, partially lit by a large moon, which appeared swollen against the navy blue sky. The phone rang again. Bevan very nearly didn't answer it. 'Hello,' she sighed into the receiver.

'May I speak with Andy,' a voice snapped back at her, no attempt at pleasantries. It was Carol Calder.

Some ingrained instinct made Dani reply, without hesitation, 'I'm afraid you've just missed him. I'm sorry for keeping him so late, but he's on his way home now.'

Carol grunted, 'okay, thanks.' Then the line went dead.

Dani snatched up her mobile and hit the speed dial. The phone she was calling rang onto voice mail. 'Andy? It's Bevan here. I don't know where the hell you are but Carol just called my flat thinking you were with me. I've told her you're on your way home. She'll be expecting you in twenty minutes time.' Dani took a deep breath. 'I'll cover for you this once, because of everything we've been through together, but never again. I hope that's understood.'

Chapter 16

It turned out that Tony Lomond had no alibi. He'd gone for drinks with some of the lads from the rowing club early on the Saturday evening but then returned to his flat near to the university campus and spent the rest of the night there alone.

Bevan couldn't yet rule him out as a suspect. Lomond had been ordered to remain in the city. The DCI had instructed a couple of DCs to keep him under surveillance. All he'd done in the previous twenty four hours was move between his home and the university library. No one else coming or going from the flat. Dani found this suspicious in itself.

Bevan had the case files spread out across her desk when Professor Morgan was shown to her office. The man was tall and bearded, with piercing blue eyes. Dani placed him in his early sixties.

She held out her hand as he entered.

The professor seemed to hesitate for a moment before he took it. He appeared almost reluctant to make physical contact. Dani put him down as one of those self-contained academic types.

'Thank you for coming Professor Morgan,' she began with a warm smile. 'Please take a seat.'

'Not at all, I'm happy to help the police with their enquiries.'

Dani wheeled her chair closer, so that there wasn't a desk between them. 'Is this your first time consulting with the City Division?'

Morgan nodded. 'I've been on the list for six months, but hadn't been contacted in that time.'

'We don't get many cases which require your kind of specialist input, thank goodness.'

'I imagine not. But you have now?'

'Before I set out the details, I need to remind you that whatever is discussed here remains strictly confidential.'

'Of course. I was once a practising psychologist. I understand the importance of confidentiality.' Morgan clasped his large hands together in an expectant gesture.

Dani reached behind her and selected the photograph of Nathan McLaren. She handed it to the professor. 'Have you seen the accounts of this man's murder on the news?'

'Yes, I have. The unfortunate chap's body was discovered in Balgray Reservoir, is that right?'

'Correct.' The DCI outlined the details of the case that they'd ascertained so far. She handed him the file.

Morgan nodded his head as he listened, saying nothing throughout. Then he read the report in silence for what felt like hours to the DCI.

Eventually, Dani said, 'we have no reason to believe we are dealing with a serial offender here, but my DS felt you may have some insights to offer, what with your research into Ian Cummings' crimes.'

The professor pursed his lips. 'Do you recall the west London murders, DCI Bevan? You would have been very young when they occurred.'

'I don't remember very much from the time. I was at school on Colonsay back then. I have skimmed the reports since, however.'

'Then you'll know that the popular press called Cummings the 'latch-key killer.' This was because he got hold of the keys to his victims' flats, letting himself in and waiting for them to arrive back home from work. The murders themselves were brutal and frenzied. The characteristics were quite different from the case you've got here.'

'I suppose the reason we wanted your advice was because of the possible homosexual element to the crime.' Dani felt she was being placed on the back foot by this man. His attitude seemed almost hostile. 'In your expert opinion, from what you've read, do you think McLaren's sexuality would have played a significant part in his death?'

'It's what took him out of the comfort of his own home on that Saturday evening, even though he must have been exhausted after attending the Fair. It was also most certainly the reason for him being in Balgray Park, so I'd say it was absolutely central.'

'What was Ian Cummings' motive to kill those young men?'

Morgan tipped his head to one side and looked thoughtful. 'The man is undoubtedly a psychopath. I've interviewed Cummings on a number of occasions and he shows no remorse or appreciation of his crimes. He is one of those individuals for whom that part of the brain which allows us to feel empathy for others does not function. Having said that, Ian did have a justification of sorts for the murders. I find that they always do.' The professor stared off into the distance, gazing over Dani's shoulder and out of the window. 'As a boy, Cummings had lived in a number of care homes. In each of these institutions he was sexually assaulted by the older boys, many of whom were not much younger than his victims. This was where the rage had come from.'

'Did Cummings know any of the men he killed?'

'He'd picked them all up in bars at some point in the months before the murders. He always insisted he went back to their flats for sex. This was how Cummings was able to take an imprint of their door keys. Eventually, it was how he was caught. The police knew he was prowling the gay bars and nightclubs of Soho for his victims. They set up a kind of sting operation – a honey-trap, if you like.'

'We believe that Nathan McLaren may have picked up the man who killed him in one of Glasgow's gay bars.'

'Of course, you have CCTV cameras these days, which the Metropolitan police working in London in the late 80s did not. Those officers had to rely upon hundreds of painstakingly garnered witness statements. There was also the issue that many of the detectives themselves felt a few less homosexuals on the streets of the city might not be such a bad thing. Times were rather different then.'

'Luckily, no one on my team feels like that now, otherwise, they wouldn't be on my team any longer.' Dani was becoming increasingly frustrated with this man and was finding it hard to keep the emotion out of her voice.

'You want to know my professional observations on the circumstances of this particular murder.' Morgan rubbed at the grey hairs on his chin. 'I suspect that the killing of Nathan McLaren was carefully planned. It's *possible* the murderer lost his temper on the spur of the moment, beating and smothering McLaren, then, realising what he had done, used a bin bag from the boot of his car to dispose of the body. However, certain elements in the PM report suggest the act was more organised than that, most notably, the wedding ring found in McLaren's gullet. The man was either forced to swallow it or the article was shoved down his throat after death. Whichever is the case, it's a sign. The killer has left us a message. It's up to us to decipher what this message means.'

'What do *you* think it means?'

Morgan narrowed his bright blue eyes. 'There are several possibilities. The killer may have been forced to swallow objects as part of some kind of childhood abuse and is regaining a sense of power by repeating the act on someone else. Or, the use of the wedding ring is deeply symbolic. The perpetrator may have been raped or assaulted by a married man. He might have targeted Nathan for this specific reason.'

Bevan jotted these two theories down.

'Most importantly,' Morgan waggled a long finger at the DCI. 'We should bear in mind that the person who committed this crime may not themselves be gay.'

Dani stopped writing and looked up.

'There is no evidence that the killer actually had intercourse with McLaren. Penetration *had* taken place, but potentially with a foreign object, as yet unfound. This could mean that the motive wasn't sexual at all. In the case of Ian Cummings, the victims had been raped repeatedly before and after death. This murder has a more *clinical* feel to it.'

'So, we might be heading along a blind alley by assuming this murder resulted from Nathan's homosexuality?'

Professor Morgan raised his hands in the air. 'Psychology is not an exact science, Detective Chief Inspector. I cannot promise that is the case. All I can do is to provide you with my opinion. But if I were you, I'd look at everyone connected with McLaren, not just his lovers. The family and friends must be suspects too.'

Dani nodded, feeling slightly deflated. This advice widened rather than narrowed their search. But something about this man's instincts seemed to ring true. When they had more evidence to go on, she would certainly be looking him up again.

Chapter 17

Andy Calder was doing his best to keep a low profile at work. He'd volunteered to sift through the CCTV footage from the gay bars of Sauchiehall Street on the afternoon of Saturday, 25th July. It was a long and tedious task but kept him away from the DCI for a few hours longer.

Calder could see his boss was still deep in conversation with that shrink in her office, the guy who looked like Gandalf from the Lord of the Rings but wearing an ill-fitting, shabby suit. So when the phone rang on Phil's desk and there was no one else around, Andy strode over to answer it.

It was the lassie from reception, informing him that Ewan McLaren was down in the lobby, waiting to speak to someone from the investigation team. Calder sighed and picked up his jacket, heading for the lift.

'What can I do for you, sonny?' Andy laid a hand on the boy's shoulder, noting how awful he looked. His hair was lank and greasy and it was clear he'd not slept in days. 'Come on.'

The detective led Ewan into one of the family rooms, asking the desk sergeant to sort them out a couple of teas with plenty of sugar. He sat opposite the lad, waiting for him to start the conversation.

'I've done nothing but go over stuff in my head these last few days. I can't help but think that you must have got it wrong about Dad – him meeting up with gay men, I mean.' Ewan seemed to be struggling not to cry.

'I'm sorry, Ewan, but the evidence is very clear cut. Your Dad was seeing a therapist about his feelings. The situation is well documented. Your mother even knew about it.'

The boy shuffled forward in his seat. 'But for the last few months, I actually thought Dad might have another woman on the go. Whenever we went out anywhere together, he was always pointing out the good-looking girls. It was so out of character I thought that maybe he was having some kind of mid-life crisis. Don't you see? The lassies he was picking out were really fit – the kinds of girls I fancied too. So he couldn't have been gay, could he? Not for real, otherwise he wouldn't have known which were the pretty ones?'

Andy sighed. 'It's what's called, throwing up a blind. He was trying to put you off the scent. I expect your dad really didn't want you and your brother to find out that he was gay.' Calder suddenly had a memory flash. He pictured his Uncle Donny in one of the dingy rock venues of Glasgow in the mid-nineties, nudging his young nephew whenever a bonny girl went by, winking exaggeratedly, playing up to his jack-the-lad image. The thought made Andy feel deeply uncomfortable.

The tears had finally escaped onto Ewan's cheeks. 'I know you're probably right, but if that's the case why didn't he just tell me? I can understand him not telling Cormac, he's just a silly kid. But I would have listened. I'm not some kind of bigot. I knew my parents weren't happy, I'm not blind. Dad didn't need to run around in secret and get himself bloody killed!'

The lad was sobbing by this stage and Andy held him in his arms. 'It wasn't as easy for your father as that. You were his son and he loved you to pieces.

He didn't want to shatter the image you'd built up of him. Believe me, Ewan, you were the *last* person your dad wanted to tell.'

The boy nodded, his head half buried in Calder's shoulder. Andy thought that finally, the lad seemed to be taking it on board.

*

When Andy returned to his desk, the professor had gone and his boss was in the office by herself. He took a deep breath and walked over, knocking lightly on the door.

As Calder entered, Dani gestured towards the chair in front of her. 'Take a seat.'

'I'd like to explain, about the other night.'

Dani shook her head. 'You don't need to. I've made some mistakes in my own private life, some of which you've bailed me out of. I can hardly start pointing the finger at others.' The DCI sighed heavily. 'However, I can't bear to see you scupper your future with Carol and Amy. *Please* think carefully about whatever it is you're doing.'

Andy nodded, the colour draining from his cheeks. This was worse than the bollocking he'd been expecting. 'I don't know if I feel the same about Carol any longer.' The words came out as a hoarse whisper.

Calder saw a flash of anger pass across Dani's dark eyes. 'That's the sex talking. But once the initial lust has blown itself out between you and this woman, what's left? I've been there, Andy. I know what I'm talking about. This case has brought back the memory of what happened to your uncle and it's messing with your head. Stop seeing her. I'm begging you, as a good friend.'

Andy avoided her gaze. 'I know you mean well,

boss, but I'm not sure I can promise you that.'

Dani felt a wave of sadness wash over her. 'Fine. Then we'll say no more about it.'

Chapter 18

The meal went more smoothly than Andy thought it would. Mae had prepared a full roast dinner with all the trimmings, even though it was a really warm day. Gavin even had to open the French doors, so that the light breeze could cool them as they sat around the table.

Andy was pleased to have a chance to see John again. The lad was tall and lean with a thin, handsome face. Calder would have liked his cousin to resemble Donny a bit more. The similarities were definitely there, around the eyes mostly, but Andy had to concede that John was more like Mae's side of the family.

'How are you finding college?' Carol asked politely, whilst she dished up a miniature plateful for Amy.

'I'm really enjoying it, thanks,' John replied. 'I wasn't sure at first if I'd made the right decision, but now I'm really glad I chose to stay in Glasgow.'

'That's because you've met Shiona,' Lizzie put in. She leant down to address the wee girl next to her. 'She's John's girlfriend.'

Amy began to giggle.

Luckily, the young man took his sister's joshing in good humour. 'Shiona would have loved to have come along today but she's up near Loch Lomond with her parents this week.'

'I'm sure we'll meet her again,' Carol said.

Gavin's attitude had softened considerably since Andy's last visit. The presence of Carol and Amy seemed to make him much more comfortable. The men lapsed into a good-natured discussion about the prospects for St Columba Football Club in the forthcoming premiership season.

Andy noticed that Mae remained quiet throughout lunch. When they'd finished eating, he stood up to help their hostess clear the plates from the table. Gavin led the guests out the back. He'd just had a summer house constructed that he wanted to show Carol. Andy could see, from the kitchen window, his daughter running madly across the huge lawn. Andy felt the pang of guilt he often experienced when in other people's large houses that they didn't have a garden of their own for her to play in.

When she knew the others were out of earshot, Mae turned towards Andy. 'I don't want to hurt Gavin.'

'I'm not sure why the hell you married the guy. He's clearly not in your league.' Andy placed the cutlery in the dishwasher with a clatter.

'I love him.'

Calder stopped what he was doing, the words hanging heavy in the air between them.

'*Come on*,' Mae gasped in frustration. 'Don't try and tell me you don't love Carol. I wouldn't believe you for a second.'

Andy straightened up and took her by the shoulders. 'But it's different for us. I don't remember ever feeling like this.'

Mae wriggled about, as if she was trying to shake herself free of his grasp. 'You're getting your emotions muddled up. It's the excitement of possessing something that your beloved uncle once had that's intoxicating you. It's got nothing to do with me, not really.'

Calder frowned. 'How can you say that – when you know what it's like when we're making love?'

'It's an illusion and it will pass. When you get to

my age you've learnt that much at least.'

Andy squeezed more tightly. 'I'm not some naive wee bairn. I know what I'm feeling.'

Mae tried to take a step away from him and caught her bare leg on the door of the dishwasher. A trickle of crimson blood rolled down to her ankle.

'Is everything okay, Mum?' The question travelled towards them from the open doorway. John Calder was standing there, silhouetted against the lowering afternoon sun.

'Oh it's fine. I've just stumbled backwards and grazed my leg.'

'Let me see.' The young man moved across and plucked a sheet of kitchen paper from the roll, proceeding to dab at the tiny cut. He twisted his body round and peered up at Andy. 'I'll deal with this. You can go out and join Carol and Amy now.' The words were not delivered as a suggestion but stated coldly, not inviting a reply.

Andy said nothing, brushing past the pair of them and heading out into the garden, his mind racing with unwelcome thoughts. He tried to focus his attention on Amy instead, who was still running in endless circles around the grass, her arms waving in the air. Carol was standing in the summer house, deep in conversation with Gavin. Calder jogged towards his daughter and scooped her up, swinging her high into the blue sky until she was shrieking with laughter and begging him to stop.

Chapter 19

Dani thought the guy in the interview room was probably in his early twenties. His hair was cropped short at the sides but left a little longer on top so it could be gelled up into what could only be described as a quiff. His sleeveless top revealed the tattoo of a bird of paradise on his tanned upper arm.

DC Laidlaw had brought the man into the station to make a statement. The detective thought his superior might want to hear what he had to say.

Bevan knocked on the door and opened it. Laidlaw stood up as she entered and pulled out a chair. 'Paul Black, this is DCI Danielle Bevan. If you could just repeat for her what you just told me, I'd be most grateful.'

Black sat upright, not with nervousness but determination. 'Pleased to meet you, DCI Bevan. I'd been wondering whether to come into the station and speak with someone, but then the police officers arrived this morning at the salon on Rose Street, where I work. They beat me to it.'

'What information do you have for us, Mr Black?'

'I knew Nathan McLaren. Not particularly well, but enough to share a couple of drinks with him for the evening. He was a really nice guy.'

'How did you come into contact with Mr McLaren?' Dani leaned forward with interest.

'Nathan was in Bacchus one lunchtime, we got chatting then. He'd not been out long. We arranged to have drinks that Friday night, as he didn't know many guys on the Glasgow scene.'

'What date was this, do you recall?'

Paul puckered his lips. 'It must have been the first weekend in July, because I was out of town the following Saturday. My sister lives in Balloch and she's just had a bairn.'

'Did you know that Nathan was married to a woman?'

Paul looked sad. 'No, he didn't mention that and I never noticed him wear a ring. I wouldn't have encouraged him if I'd known; whether he was married to a man or a woman. He should have come clean to his wife first. No one deserves to be two-timed.'

Dani got the sense that Paul had probably been on the receiving end of such treatment himself. 'Were you having a relationship with Nathan?'

Paul seemed surprised by the question. 'No! Nathan was decades older than me, not my type at all. We'd just become mates, that's all.'

It was Bevan's turn to appear puzzled. 'Then what do you have to tell us?'

The man leaned in closer. Dani could smell his tangy aftershave. 'The Friday evening we met for drinks at the Oyster Bar, Nathan got talking to this chap. They were getting on really well, so I slunk off to join a group of other folk I knew. Nathan came back over later, when this man had gone. I teased him about it and Nathan admitted they'd exchanged numbers. When I saw the report about Nathan's murder on the news and how they were saying he was married with kids and no mention of him being gay, I thought that I'd better inform the police of what I knew.'

'Could you provide us with a description of this man, so that we can create an E-fit?'

Paul nodded. 'Yeah, of course. I'll do my best. I can tell you now that he was really good-looking, that's why I was ribbing Nathan so much. I was joking how I'd been on the scene for years and never got the number of a guy who was such a hunk.' He looked suddenly wistful. 'We had a laugh that evening. When we parted, I promised to call his mobile and arrange another night out, but then I had to go to my sister's and got caught up in other shit, you know? The next thing, I hear Nathan's body's been found dumped in the reservoir. I felt really bad.'

'Well, if your description can help us to locate this other man, then you will have done something important to help your friend.'

Paul's expression brightened. 'Yeah, I suppose I would.'

*

DC Alice Mann stared hard at the E-fit. The chiselled features of the face staring back at her certainly felt vaguely familiar.

'Could this be Tony Lomond?' DCI Bevan pressed. 'You've seen the man more often than the rest of us.'

Alice shook her fine bob of light brown hair. 'There's a resemblance, but I really couldn't say for certain. Maybe we could get Lomond back in to do a line up – see if this Paul Black can pick him out?'

'I've not got enough evidence for that. Even if Lomond spent an entire evening having a tête a tête with Nathan three weeks ago, it doesn't put him directly in the frame for the murder. We already knew they met on the pub circuit.'

'But Paul Black's account makes their liaison sound like it was more than friendship. Lomond has always denied that. It shows he was lying.'

'*If* we're talking about the same man.'

Alice looked apologetic. 'I can't give you a definite

answer from this picture. If anything, I'd say this likeness was of someone older. A man in his mid to late thirties, perhaps?'

Dani smiled sadly. 'That was Paul Black's assessment too. He thought the man who was chatting Nathan up was mid-thirties, at the very least.' Bevan took back the print-out. 'Well, it's going into the bulletin this afternoon and I may get a slot on the six o'clock news. DCS Nicholson is looking into it.'

'Great, that should generate a decent response from the public. We *are* getting somewhere with this, Ma'am. I can feel it.'

Chapter 20

Bevan had been required to deliver a lot of bad news in her career, but this particular conversation she was absolutely dreading. They'd received a call from the East Renfrewshire Constabulary late that afternoon. Only a handful of officers were left on their floor at headquarters. The DC she spoke to then e-mailed over a series of photographs. Bevan had printed them off and was carrying them in her briefcase right now.

Dani approached the building and pressed on the buzzer. It was Carol's voice that crackled over the intercom.

'It's DCI Bevan, may I come up?'

The external door clicked open. Dani pushed through and mounted the stairs. When she reached the top, the door to the Calders' flat was already ajar. Bevan hoped to God that Andy was in there. The DCI wasn't sure she could face Carol alone, not knowing what she did about her husband.

It was Andy who was standing in the doorway waiting for her. He looked strange, his expression distant. 'Has there been a development in the case, Ma'am?'

'Yes,' Dani answered, following her colleague into the kitchen.

Andy automatically poured her out a glass of wine. He reached for his own half-drunk beer and sat at the table opposite Bevan. 'Have you had a response to the E-fit?'

'Not yet. But the bobbies from East Renfrewshire have found something, out at Balgray Park.'

'I didn't know they had any teams still searching for evidence over there.' Andy's posture visibly stiffened.

'They don't. But some keen young DC decided to act on her own initiative. Whilst off duty, she took her dog for a walk down to the weir. The DC knew there was a piece of wire mesh stretched across the water that stopped unwanted debris from getting caught in the mechanism of the dam. It's a quarter of a mile downstream from the place where McLaren's body was dumped. She had a hunch there might be something caught in there.'

'What did she find?' Andy's face was unreadable.

'There was another bin bag, snagged in the mesh. The team at Barrhead took photographs of the items inside it before they were sent off to forensics. Jenny McLaren has already confirmed that the wallet, phone and keys in the bag were Nathan's. But there's other stuff too - things that Jenny couldn't identify. I'm sorry, but I need to ask if you recognise anything.' Dani took a sip of wine. 'Of course, you don't need to look. I can take the pictures over to Mae Mortimer and show them to her instead. I just knew you'd want to be informed first.'

Andy lowered his gaze. 'Thanks. I'm glad you came to me. I'll do it.' He sipped reluctantly from his glass, as if to fortify himself for the ordeal that was to come but realising he couldn't stomach it.

Dani brought the Perspex folder out of her briefcase. She spread the photographs on the table between them.

Carol had come to stand in the doorway. She said nothing, seeming to understand what was going on without having to be told. Andy spent several minutes eyeing the high resolution images. Each one showed tables laid out with various battered objects, some obviously older than others. His vision lingered on one of the shots. With an enormous effort of willpower, Andy pulled it towards him.

'That's Donny's ring.' He tapped the picture with a shaky finger. 'He wore it as a kind of joke, really. Don bought it at a Twisted Sister gig in New York. It's got a skull worked into the silver band. If the techies look closely, they should see the date and venue of the gig engraved onto the back. It was some time in the mid-eighties, at the Apollo, I think.'

Dani nodded, saying nothing. She began to gather the photos back into a pile.

'What does this mean?' Andy looked at her with wide, pleading eyes.

The DCI addressed him as she would any other frightened, bewildered relative. 'It means that whoever killed Nathan McLaren was very likely involved in the disappearance of your uncle ten years ago. That's all we can say for certain at this stage.'

'I want you to search the reservoir for more bodies.' Andy looked resolute, defiant.

'Of course,' Dani replied. 'I will get onto the DCS first thing in the morning.'

*

The team were gathered before her. They were quieter and more solemn than usual. Calder was in a discussion with DCS Nicholson upstairs, so Dani could speak freely.

'East Renfrewshire have sent the items from the black bag they found in the weir away for analysis. We're hoping to be able to extract DNA from some of the items. There's a watch, for example, which may have hairs caught in the strap.'

'Do we have any idea how old the items are?' Phil

Boag asked.

'Well, we know that Donald Calder's ring has been missing for ten years. But I'd suggest that a couple of the other items in that bag were even older than that.'

Alice Mann put up her hand. 'If we believe that the person who killed McLaren was also involved in the disappearance of Andy's uncle, that puts Tony Lomond out of the frame, surely? He would have only been twenty years old back then and he studied for his first degree in Aberdeen.'

Dani nodded. 'This discovery changes the whole complexion of the McLaren case, I'd agree.'

Phil furrowed his brow. 'Both men went missing on the last Saturday in July. That's a holiday for all schools and universities. Lomond would surely have been back at home with his parents in the Glasgow area on that date in 2005.'

'It's something we'll have to check out. For the time being, the focus is on what the divers discover at the bottom of the Balgray Reservoir.'

Dan Clifton visibly shuddered. 'My running club use the Balgray Country Park. It's pretty unsettling to know it could be a dump site for a serial killer.'

'We don't know if that's what we're dealing with yet,' Bevan said sternly. 'Until we can ascertain that Donald Calder is actually dead, we continue to consider him a missing person. None of this gets out to the press, okay?'

The officers nodded, Bevan tried to make eye contact with them all, to be sure of their cooperation. 'We have a date which connects these two men – Donny Calder and Nathan McLaren. What was it about the Glasgow Fair Saturday that precipitated their disappearance? *This* factor is what we concentrate on. I want lists of all the stall holders, ice-cream salesmen and fairground operators who were on Glasgow Green this year *and* back in 2005.'

Alice rolled her eyes at the vast nature of the task.

'I know it won't be easy. But this is the key to finding our man. I'm certain of it.'

Chapter 21

DCI Bevan and DS Phil Boag pressed the doorbell of a grand Victorian villa situated in the heart of a quiet suburb of Paisley.

Mae Mortimer answered quickly, as if she'd been waiting for them to arrive. The woman led the officers through the house to a light, airy kitchen. She put on the kettle as if on autopilot.

Dani intercepted her tea-making routine by placing a hand on her arm, guiding Mae towards one of the dining chairs. 'Is your husband at home?'

Mae shook her head. 'Gavin's at work.'

'Okay. Would you like us to call him home before we explain things to you?'

'No. It's got nothing to do with my husband, not really. It's the kids who should be here to find out what happened to their dad.'

'I was thinking more of having someone around who could provide you with moral support.'

'I'm fine.' She leant forward, her eyes wide and pleading. 'Just tell me, *please*. I've waited so long for news.'

Dani took a deep breath. 'The divers searching the Balgray Reservoir found another body. It had been wrapped in polythene sheeting and weighted down with rocks and other debris.'

'Is it him?' Mae gripped Dani's arm.

'All that remains is the skeleton and some fragments of clothing. It's going to take a little time, but our pathologist believes he'll be able to provide us with this person's height, sex and build. Possibly even their age. We *will* be able to confirm one way or the other if this is Donald. There will be closure, Mrs

Mortimer, I promise.'

The woman gasped, throwing her head back and allowing the tears to roll unchecked down her cheeks. 'We can bury him at last. You don't know how that feels, DCI Bevan.'

'No, but I can imagine.'

Phil brought a cup of sweet tea over to the table and placed it in front of her. 'We have the transcripts of the original interviews that you gave the police ten years ago, but would you be prepared to answer a few more questions for us now?'

Mae turned her gaze towards him, dabbing at her eyes with a tissue. 'What do you want to know?'

Phil took a seat and cleared his throat. 'Were you and your husband getting on well at the time of his disappearance?'

'What's this?' Mae snapped. 'A re-run of the original, pathetic excuse for an investigation? Isn't it finally clear that Don didn't run off with some other woman?'

'Yes, it is clear,' Dani continued. 'But now it is also plain that whoever murdered Nathan McLaren also murdered your husband. It is our firm belief that Nathan was targeted as a victim because of his homosexuality.'

Bevan had expected Mae to look shocked, angry even, at hearing this statement. Instead, her body seemed to crumple with relief. 'I didn't ever know if that was a factor in his disappearance, that's why I never said anything. It would have destroyed Don's family and deeply upset the kids if it had come out.'

Dani waited for her to continue.

'When we first got together, Don told me he was bisexual. He'd never kept that side of his sexuality a secret from me. But his own family were a different matter. They're not exactly very tolerant of that kind of thing.'

Dani thought about Andy and immediately recognised what she was talking about.

'He'd had a couple of boyfriends in his early twenties. I knew one of them quite well. But Don always said he *loved* me, that I was the one he wanted to spend the rest of his life with. We were happy for a long time, certainly when the kids came along and they were little. But about a year before he went missing, Don had become withdrawn and depressed. I never knew if it had anything to do with his feelings towards men, I was too frightened to ask. By the July of 2005, Don and I were barely having sex at all. I suppose it was always crazy for me to have believed he'd be able to give up that side of his life and then expect him to be happy about it.'

'You loved each other, what else were you supposed to do?'

Mae nodded, sensing that the detective understood. 'A part of me thought that Andy's dad was right and Don had got drunk that night and thrown himself into the river. But there was always that niggling doubt in my mind. Don would never have deliberately left Lizzie and John, you see – not without saying goodbye in some way. He would have left a note at least.'

'Could Don have been meeting somebody that evening – a man he'd come into contact with at the Fair?'

Mae shrugged. 'It's possible. I've re-run that whole day in my head thousands of times. No one was behaving out of the ordinary. As far as I was concerned, Don may have been battling with his urges towards men, but he'd never acted on them.'

Dani reached out and laid her hand on Mae's shoulder. 'Thank you. That's all the questions we have for now. I'll let you know about any information we receive with regards to the identification of the remains we've found.'

Mae stood up awkwardly as the officers made to leave. 'Will DC Andy Calder be working on the case?'

Bevan paused. 'No, I'm afraid he's been given leave for the duration of this investigation. He is too close to the situation, you see.'

The woman gave a taut smile. 'He won't like that much.'

Dani smiled back. 'No, I expect he won't like that at all.'

Chapter 22

On his second visit to the Pitt Street Headquarters, Bevan had decided to introduce Professor Morgan to the rest of the team. Dani felt the man had made a better attempt at smartening up his appearance for this consultation. The suit he was wearing looked like it might have been new.

'I've provided Professor Morgan with the case files and the evidence we've gathered so far. He has kindly agreed to provide us with some feedback on the type of perpetrator we may be looking for.'

The Professor took a step forward. He was more comfortable standing in front of a packed lecture theatre than he was during one-to-one encounters. This type of situation suited him well. 'When DCI Bevan first spoke to me about this case, I believed that the field was genuinely open as to who might have been Nathan's killer. With the discovery of a second body, at the same dump site as the first and the bag full of 'trophies' from other victims, the crime takes on a whole new significance.' He pointed to the photographs taken of the skeletal remains discovered at the bottom of Balgray Reservoir. 'The DCI informs me that the skeleton recovered is that of a male in his late thirties to early forties, of roughly 5'11" in height. This person had at one time broken a nose and had it reset. They had also, pre-puberty, fractured the radius bone of the left arm. Using Donald Calder's medical records, we can now confirm categorically that this is him.'

One of the officers let out a gasp, muttering, 'poor Andy.'

Morgan nodded sympathetically. 'Although in

these cases, I usually find that the families are gratified to finally have a body to bury. After ten years with no attempt to make contact of any kind, even with his children, it was obvious that the man was dead.'

Dani was glad that Andy wasn't here to listen to such a clinical account of his uncle's fate.

'The connecting factor in these murders,' Morgan continued, 'was the men's homosexuality. We cannot now ascertain a cause of death for Donald Calder, although amongst the bones was found his wedding ring. We cannot prove it, but it seems likely that it was swallowed by the victim, as in the case of Nathan McLaren. This is what we would call a 'marker'. It is an unusual act by the perpetrator which gives us an insight into what makes them tick.'

Alice put up her hand. 'Do we *really* think it's the same killer – after ten years have passed with no other murders in between?'

'I would say there is a question mark over whether these are the only killings. That bag contained many items. It seems the Calder and McLaren families could not identify them all.'

'Then where are the other bodies? Why haven't these people been reported missing?'

'This killer may have more than one dump site,' Morgan counted points off on his fingers. 'The other victims may have had no family or friends to report them missing.'

'Or our perpetrator might move about from place to place,' Bevan interrupted. 'These murders both occurred during the Fair weekend. The man we are looking for may be itinerant and only resident in certain cities at certain times of the year. It's something my officers are already looking into.'

Morgan nodded cautiously. 'I agree. That's

definitely an avenue you need to pursue. However...' The man glanced over his shoulder at the photographs of the reservoir. 'I can't help but feel that this person knows the Glasgow area well. How would an outsider be aware that Balgray would make a good dump site?'

'If our man examined the local maps carefully enough, it would simply be an obvious choice, wouldn't it?' Alice chipped in.

Morgan spun on his heels to address her directly. 'But that kind of intelligent pre-meditation doesn't really fit with your profile of an itinerant fairground operative, does it? Crimes committed by those types of ill-educated offender are opportunist, brutal and the body dumps will be close to the murder scene, if they bother to hide the corpse at all. *This* person takes items from their victim, personal keepsakes, the bodies are carefully and intelligently disposed of.'

'Then why dump his souvenirs in the reservoir too?' Alice suddenly asked. 'Why are we finding Calder's belongings now, after all these years?'

Morgan considered this for a moment. 'You weren't meant to find McLaren's body. This would have made the killer uncomfortable. Perhaps it caused them to believe it wasn't safe to keep these trophies at home any longer.'

'Which suggests to me,' Phil put in, 'that this killer thinks someone might search their home.'

'Or they live with a person who may get suspicious after having seen McLaren's body dredged up on the news,' Dan Clifton added, 'and could start snooping around.'

'Tony Lomond,' Alice blurted out. 'He knows he's one of our main suspects. He certainly wouldn't want to have any incriminating items hanging about in his flat. We could raise a warrant to search it at any time.'

'What do you think, Professor? Could a man as young as twenty have killed Donald Calder and disposed of his body?' Dani addressed the academic directly.

He shook his head of shaggy grey hair. 'It would be highly unlikely, but nothing is outside the realms of possibility. The lad would have needed significant body strength to overpower a well-built man of 41 years old.'

'He *is* a rower, which requires building considerable upper body muscle,' Alice put in. 'I could find out if he started the sport when still at university in Aberdeen?'

'It's worth checking out,' Bevan agreed.

'Well, if you actually *want* my opinion, DCI Bevan, after inviting me all the way over here,' the professor interrupted gruffly. 'This Lomond character doesn't fit the profile. You are looking for someone who would now be in their forties or fifties, but who is still physically fit. This man is reasonably well educated but not a perennial student. Their background would prohibit such a lifestyle. Your perpetrator may do a blue collar job, but nothing too high flying. They might be self-employed or semi-skilled. He's the sort of chap who could slip under the radar easily during a police inquiry.'

'Would you write that up into a report for me?'

'Of course. My role as an expert advisor requires no less.'

Dani noticed Alice Mann make a face at the man's pomposity. She chose to ignore it. 'Thank you very much for your input, Professor. You've really helped to move the investigation forward.' She swiftly disbanded the meeting, instructing her officers to continue with their tasks and escorted Professor Morgan across the office floor towards the lift.

Chapter 23

In his more rational moments, Calder was perfectly aware that he couldn't continue to work on the case now that Don's body had been found. But he was still as mad as hell.

Carol had taken Amy out to the shops. Andy was prowling around the flat like a big cat denied access to its prey. He'd sifted through his Dad's old photograph albums for hours already, finding no evidence or indication of what it was that had led his uncle into the situation that brought about his death.

Suddenly, Andy made up his mind to do something more pro-active. He grabbed a jacket from the hallway and jogged down the steps to the communal car-park, jumping into his hatch-back and heading out of the city.

Calder thumped on the front door of the Mortimer residence, the noise causing the man working in his front garden next door to stand up straight and eye Andy suspiciously. The neighbour continued to glower at him as Mae allowed Andy to step inside.

'I assume you've heard the news?' He said bluntly.

'Yes. DCI Bevan came to see me yesterday.' Mae turned away from him and walked into the kitchen, not inviting her guest to follow, but resignedly expecting he would.

Andy trailed along at her heels. 'I expect the DCI was very kind and considerate when she told you. She's good at all that empathetic shit.'

'She was, and I believe she meant it.' Mae filled

the kettle and switched it on. 'Look, Andy, I know you're upset and angry.'

Calder let out a hollow laugh. 'I've just found out that my uncle was brutally murdered by a killer who targets gays. Then, the woman who begged me to make love to her, dug her nails into my back imploring for me not to stop, never to leave her, has cut me off without even a word, an explanation.'

Mae raised her eyes to meet his. 'I'm sorry. When you came back to see us again, on the Saturday evening of the Glasgow Fair, it was as if Don had walked in through that door once more.' She reached out to touch his cheek. 'You are so like him now, the resemblance was frightening. I wanted to feel his arms around me just that one last time. But the truth was that the sex was never like that with Don, not towards the end. He loved me, of course, but he lusted after men. I'd always know that, in my heart.'

Andy shook his head violently. 'That isn't true. All relationships cool off, especially after the kids come along. It doesn't mean Donny was a *homosexual*.'

Mae stepped forward. 'He'd had boyfriends, Andy. It was a side of his life he never discussed with your Dad, because he knew he wouldn't understand and it would hurt him. Then, he decided to settle down with me, so it didn't matter anymore. Or so we thought.'

This time it was Andy who stumbled backwards. 'And you didn't think to tell the police about this fact when he went missing?'

Mae sighed. 'It was the *last* thing I wanted to tell anybody about at that time. Can you imagine how your dad would have reacted?'

'It would have killed him,' Andy muttered.

'I didn't have any reason to believe Don's sexuality was related to him going missing.'

'The investigating officers need to know every

detail.' He sighed, 'although, those numpties who were on Don's case wouldn't have known what to do with the information anyway. It would have given them even more reason to write him off.'

'For what it's worth, I'm sorry. I really hope you and Carol can be happy. She's a lovely person – not caught up in all this shit from our past. Set yourself free of it now, Andy. Get on with your life.'

Calder abruptly looked up, as if he'd not listened to a word she'd just said. 'Can you find a pad and pen?'

Mae nodded.

'I want you to list down all the places Don had been to in the days and weeks leading up to that Glasgow Fair weekend in 2005. I don't care how trivial it might seem – trips to the supermarket, school concerts, any single damn thing that springs into your mind.'

The woman did not reply but rushed off to do exactly as she was told.

*

When Dani entered the police station in Barrhead, she was impressed by how efficiently she was escorted up to the Criminal Investigation Department. A bald man, with a smile as wide as his belly greeted her.

'Morning, Ma'am. I'm DI Matt Bonnar, we've spoken on the phone.'

'Pleased to meet you, Matt. I want to begin by saying how impressed I am with your work so far on the McLaren case. The discovery of that bag in the weir has changed everything. I'm looking to expand the whole operation now.'

Matt nodded. 'I've got a great team here. But you should save your praise for DC Caitlin Hendry, she was the one who had the brainwave to go back and check the dam. This is only her first case out of uniform. The lass has certainly got herself noticed.'

Bonnar led the DCI over to a workstation, where a young woman was busily tapping the keys of her computer. As the girl looked up, Dani experienced a flash of recognition. She held out her hand and smiled. 'Well done DC Hendry. A great job.'

'Thank you, Ma'am.'

'Have our paths crossed before?' Bevan asked, tipping her head to one side curiously.

'The lost wee girl at the Glasgow Fair, Ma'am - Lily. I brought her back to the parents.'

'Of course.' Dani was annoyed at herself for forgetting, but it felt like it happened years ago now. 'If your DI can spare you Caitlin, I would very much appreciate seconding you to my team at Pitt Street for the duration of this investigation. I'm a good DC down and I've got a sense you might just fill his boots quite admirably.'

Chapter 24

DCI Bevan had brought the contents of the plastic bag dumped in the reservoir back to Pitt Street. They'd been fully examined by the forensic laboratory, who'd found no fingerprints or DNA traces. The items had been in the water for nearly a week. She felt she'd been foolish to imagine there'd be any human residue left on them.

Nevertheless, Dani spread the various articles out across her desk. She looked at Donny Calder's ring first. It was tarnished to the extent that you'd never know it was silver unless you found the hallmark on the underside. Andy had been correct, next to the hallmark was inlaid the date of the Twisted Sister concert in NYC; 26th August 1984.

She set the ring back on the table and lifted the watch. It had a standard Seiko analogue face set into a black leather strap. Bevan felt this was the kind of timepiece that would be worn by a man of at least thirty. It wasn't a young person's watch. They were sending it off to an expert who had a shop in Bath Street. He would be able to place a date on it for them.

The other items were a jumble of miscellany. They had Nathan's keys, mobile phone and wallet, but nothing else there was so easily definable. Dani picked up a little carved elephant, which looked as if it had once hung on a chain. It seemed to be made out of ivory, which dated the piece from the get-go. Apart from that there were a couple of cheap gold-plated chains and another ring, this time a signet, which was smaller than Donny's – as if the owner wore it on their little finger.

Bevan would have the pieces photographed for

the local press and for their slot on Crime Scotland. It often amazed the DCI how well people could remember objects they'd not set eyes on for decades. She firmly believed they may yet be able to identify other potential victims from these items.

Dani glanced up when there was a knock at the door. It was DC Mann. She beckoned her in.

'We've been checking out the site-holders who were on Glasgow Green for the Fair weekend, Ma'am,' Alice said.

'Any joy?'

'Most of the craft and food vendors were new to the Fair this year. But a number of the ice cream vans have been trading around the Glasgow area for donkey's years. DC Clifton is going out to interview the owners today. As for the fairground, it appears to have been a different operation from the one that pitched up at the Green in 2005.'

Dani sighed. 'That's not the result we were hoping for.'

Alice referred to her notes. 'In 2005, the amusements were provided by a travelling funfair called Coco's. They were a family operation and set up on the Green with their caravans, staying for the duration of the weekend. This year, the amusements and rides were provided by a funfair hire company based in Ayr. They do all the Glasgow events.'

'Is this Coco's operation still in existence?'

'I'll look into it Ma'am. I didn't want to continue any further with this line if there was no obvious connection to the present day.'

'I'll like you to follow the lead anyway, Alice. I know that Professor Morgan was sceptical but I still think it's worth checking out.'

The DC nodded, turning to leave.

'Oh, and bring Caitlin Hendry in on the inquiry, she's young but has very good instincts. Get her doing some digging into exactly what went on at the fair back in 2005. Our new recruit may just spot something we've missed.'

Chapter 25

Donald Patrick Calder was born in the spring of 1964. His brother, Jack, was already fourteen years old and about to leave school. Donald received a better education than Andy's father, purely as a consequence of coming along when he did.

Don stayed on at school long enough to complete his Highers, joining a journalism apprenticeship scheme at one of the local papers in the early eighties. That's where Andy's uncle had remained for the rest of his short career. He covered the sports fixtures and music gigs for a small scale Paisley rag. Don might have moved onto working for the Herald one day, but if his nephew were perfectly honest, there was no sign of this at the time of Don's disappearance.

Andy stared at the list Mae had given him. For much of early 2005, Don had been researching for his book about St Columba Football Club. He'd been commissioned by the board to write it. Mae had catalogued her husband's visits to the library in Paisley and to St Columba's Park itself during the weeks before he went missing. The book wasn't set to make Don much money. It was going to be sold to raise funds for the club. According to Mae, Don had been promised a fixed fee upon completion of the project.

Donald had certainly thrown himself into the task. Andy recalled how his uncle was always talking about it. The detective realised now that it meant a great deal to Don. He'd been a writer and this was to be his first book. Andy had to blink back tears when he thought of how the man had never got the opportunity to finish it. For the first time since Don's body was discovered, it was anger that surged through Andy's veins, rather than a vague sense of confusion and disappointment. He wanted to find the bastard who did this. It didn't matter what his uncle's sexuality was, he hadn't deserved to suffer a miserable fate like that.

Carol came into the room and hovered at her husband's shoulder. 'Would you like a cuppa?' She eventually asked.

'No thanks,' Andy sighed. 'I'm going to have to go and see Dad.'

Carol observed his hunched posture and placed her arms around him, resting her face against his cheek. 'I'm sorry,' she whispered.

Andy clasped her hands, turning to face her. 'What on earth have *you* got to be sorry about?'

'I'm sorry about what happened to Don and for not really understanding how serious it was all those years ago. I didn't give you enough sympathy when your uncle first went missing. I was young and selfish and thought you should be giving all of your attention to me. What happened to Don was just awful.'

Andy kissed his wife tenderly. 'Don't you ever feel bad about this, Carol. You stood by me back then and plenty of girls wouldn't have. We'll get past this, I promise. I just need some time to deal with it in my own way.'

Carol did not reply, but buried her face into his neck and held him tight.

*

Jack Calder was wheeling a barrow full of garden waste along the front path when Andy pulled up at the kerb. His father hadn't spotted him yet and Andy was tempted to simply drive away again. Instead, he took a deep breath and opened up.

'Morning Da',' he called over the hedge.

The man put a hand to his bald pate, shading his eyes from the sun and slowly taking in his son's casual attire. 'Why aren't you at work?'

'I'm on leave.' Andy proceeded to help his father transfer the heap of clippings into a big plastic bin. 'How's Mum?'

'Aye, she'd keeping well. Are Carol and Amy okay?' Jack scrutinized his son closely, always possessing a razor-sharp instinct when it came to his children.

Andy felt his cheeks redden, but he was already flushed by the heat and exertion. He hoped it didn't show. 'They're good, aye. Amy enjoyed the trip to Troon. She spent most of her time splashing in the water.'

Jack chuckled. 'Just like your sister when she was a bairn.'

Andy laid a hand on his father's arm. 'I need to talk to you about Don.'

The older man kept his gaze fixed on the contents of the wheelbarrow. 'We've got him back now, Son. There's no more to say on the matter.'

'I've been looking into Uncle Don's movements in the days and weeks before he went missing. Did he come and see you at any point during that period?'

Jack flicked his head up. 'I don't see how knowing that would change anything. I've heard what the news reports are suggesting about my brother and this McLaren chap – about the reason why they were killed. But I don't want it discussed, especially in front of your mother or sister, is that understood? Now, go inside and say hello to your maw. She's not seen you in weeks. It's time for us to carry on with our lives now, Andy. Once the funeral's got over with, Donald Calder and his memory will be dead and gone to this family.'

Chapter 26

DC Caitlin Hendry possessed shoulder length, shaggy blonde curls which she wore twisted up into a bun for work. She used to keep her hair neatly tucked under her hat when out on the beat, but now she'd been promoted to the crime division, Caitlin was considering a more radical cut. Something like DCI Bevan's perhaps.

Hendry was enjoying working with Alice Mann. All the officers down at Barrhead had been male and at least a decade older than her. This secondment made the young DC feel she'd like to move to the city on a more long-term basis. Caitlin was certainly keen to learn whatever she could from the DCI whilst here at Pitt Street.

Caitlin spotted Alice making her way over to the desk. She swiftly pulled across her notepad so she would have her information to hand. 'How's it going?' Alice asked lightly. 'Dan is going downstairs for some cans of drink from the refectory. Do you want anything?'

'Oh, I'm okay with water, thanks.'

Alice grinned. 'You'll be the first DC at this station who isn't fuelled by Irn Bru. It makes your brain sharper, you know.'

Caitlin smiled.

'So, have you got some material for me?' Alice glanced at the pad, which was filled with copious notes.

'I've been checking out the history of this travelling fairground company, 'Coco's'. Although, to call it a company is stretching things a bit.'

Alice pulled across a seat and sat down.

'I can find evidence of Coco's being in operation way back into the sixties and maybe before. It was run by the O'Driscoll family. They were part of the travelling community who were based on a stretch of industrial land out towards East Kilbride. Did you know that the majority of Scottish 'showmen' lived on sites around Glasgow?'

The DC shook her head.

'In the early 2000s, the travelling communities were being evicted from these scraps of land, particularly when the extension to the M74 was constructed in 2003. But the O'Driscoll's were based on one of the 25 plots which had planning permission. So in 2005, they were the obvious choice to provide the entertainment for the Glasgow Fair celebrations that year.'

'Do the family still live on the same plot?'

'No,' Caitlin replied sombrely. 'They took their fairground on a tour of Europe in 2007. When they returned to Glasgow, they found their pitch had been burnt to the ground. All the static caravans were gone.'

'Was it arson?'

'The police report is inconclusive. Apparently, fires are very common on traveller sites. But the council used it as an opportunity to move the community on. The land has since been re-developed for housing.'

'So what happened to Coco's?'

'The travelling fair split up. According to a report in the Herald from 2008, the younger members of the O'Driscoll family took the rides over to Europe on a permanent basis, leaving the older members of the clan behind. The elders must have set up in camps elsewhere around Scotland. Some may even have been eligible for council housing.'

Alice sighed. 'So we've got absolutely no bloody hope of tracking any of them down now. The ones who went off abroad will be totally untraceable.'

'We've still got this hire company in Ayrshire to question. They'll be easy enough to get hold of.'

'But what's the connection between the two years – 2005 and now?' Alice said this almost to herself.

'If you don't mind, Ma'am, I'd like to do a bit more digging into this travelling fairground community and the history of the Glasgow Fair itself.'

'Go ahead,' Alice replied flatly. 'We've got no other pressing leads. And Caitlin, you really don't need to call me Ma'am, save that for the DCI.'

*

Bevan had received Professor Morgan's psychological profile report by e-mail that morning. Despite the man's ramshackle appearance, his document was methodical and well supported with evidence. Dani jotted down the man's key points. What interested the DCI, was that Morgan was still insisting that the perpetrator may not be a homosexual himself. Bevan didn't completely understand this evaluation.

Even though the idea made her cringe, Dani had picked up the phone and dialled the Professor's extension at the university. To her surprise, he seemed keen to meet the DCI to discuss his report.

They convened in a café near Kelvin Hall. Possibly because this location was closer to the Professor's own territory, he seemed more relaxed.

Dani ordered them both a coffee.

'I want to begin by thanking you for your swift response to my request.' Dani swirled a couple of sugar cubes around her cup, watching the crystals slowly dissolve.

Morgan chuckled. 'You really don't need to smooth talk me with the management speak, DCI Bevan.'

Dani glanced up in shock. 'I beg your pardon, Professor?'

A look of sadness passed across his lined face. 'I knew your mother. A very long time ago now. You are incredibly like her.'

Dani was so taken aback by this statement that she was temporarily speechless. It took several moments before her brain could even begin to consider how this could be the case.

'I was a lecturer at Aberystwyth back in the late seventies and early eighties. I had studied there too. I'm a north Walian by birth.' He smiled wistfully.

'So you and Mum studied together?' Dani's hand was shaking so much she could hardly lift her cup.

'Yes, Moira and I were undergraduates together but we stayed in touch. I was at your parents' wedding.'

'I don't remember you ever visiting the house. I know I was young, but still.'

'I only met you a couple of times. Moira and I lost touch for a while, as one does when marriage and children come along. We met up again when your mother worked at the university for a while, just after you started school.'

Dani felt her chest tightening. It was as if the professor was launching some kind of assault on her senses. Her detective's instincts were screaming at her that this man was trying to tell her something, and it was big.

'I can see that talking about your mother is making you very uncomfortable. I can stop if you wish?'

Bloody psychologists, Dani thought to herself.

This man had completely emotionally ambushed her and was now threatening to clam up. 'I'm not used to having her mentioned, Professor. My father very rarely speaks of her.'

Dani saw Morgan's mouth tighten. 'He should. Moira deserves to be remembered often. She was a remarkable woman.' He took a slow sip of his coffee. 'I went to the inquest. I wanted to talk to Huw, pass on my condolences. He wasn't even there.'

'Dad was at home with me.' Dani breathed in deeply. 'What kind of relationship did you actually have with my mother?'

'About a year before her death, I had asked Moira to marry me. We were in love with each other. She'd been very unwell ever since your birth. In my opinion, she never received proper treatment for her PND. Your father treated her like the madwoman in the attic.'

Dani stood up, her wooden chair falling backwards onto the stone tiles of the café floor. The other customers turned and stared. 'I think we'll leave it there, Professor. I'm not sure I'm interested in your *opinions* any longer.'

The man shrugged his shoulders, a gesture which angered Bevan even more. She threw a note on the table and marched straight out of the door, not allowing herself to cry until she had travelled some distance down the street.

Chapter 27

There was only one person that Dani wanted to see after leaving the café in Kelvinside. It was the middle of the day, but the pub she was now sitting in was reassuringly dingy.

Andy Calder carried a couple of drinks over to their table. He was dressed casually, in jeans and an open-necked shirt. 'There you go Ma'am, get that doon ya' neck.'

Dani chuckled, sipping the cold, white wine with relief. 'Call me Dani, you're on leave for heaven's sake.'

'Old habits die hard.'

Bevan knocked back half the glass in one go. 'It was his blatant hostility that really shook me up. His eyes were full of hatred. Why does he feel that way about me – about Dad?'

Andy rubbed at his stubbly chin. 'The professor clearly blames you for your mother turning him down. *You* would have been the reason she didn't leave to marry him. Even if I were madly in love with someone else, Amy would be the reason I stayed with Carol.'

Dani raised an eyebrow. '*Are* you madly in love with someone else?'

He smiled sadly. 'No. I don't think I'm even capable of it any more. But before you decide I'm some kind of hero, it was her who finished with me.'

'You were in a difficult place. The affair would have burnt itself out eventually. Will you tell Carol?'

'And break her into pieces? I'm not that much of a bastard.'

Dani sighed. 'Mum must have never told Dad

about her relationship with Morgan either. I knew she'd taken a job for a while. It was an administrative position, part-time, at the University of Aberystwyth. But then her mental health took a turn for the worst and she gave up. They must have continued seeing one another after she left.'

'The adult world is complicated, Dani. Your mother wasn't well and this Morgan guy may have provided her with some comfort. I don't think we could blame her for that.'

'No, I don't.' Dani polished off the rest of the wine. 'What really upset me was that the Professor was saying the stuff that's been secretly bothering me for all these years – that Dad didn't handle it right. He should have got Mum proper psychiatric help. It was obvious that Morgan thought she'd still be alive if Mum had gone away with him.' Bevan's voice broke and the tears escaped onto her face. It was the last thing she was expecting to happen.

Andy got up and moved over to place his arms around her. 'We all think that if we'd only done something differently they'd still be with us. What if Don felt he could talk to me and Dad about his sexuality? Then he wouldn't have needed go out and pick up blokes in parks at night. Maybe it's true, maybe it isn't. There's nothing we can do to change it now. We've just got to accept we messed it up and move on.'

*

The item that DS Phil Boag was carrying into her office was the very last thing Dani wanted to see that particular afternoon.

'I found it on the shelf at home, Ma'am. I thought you might want to read it, for background research.'

Bevan received the book with resignation. 'Yeah, I

probably should.' The DCI examined the front cover carefully. It showed a city scape of London by night. The title read; 'Inside the Head of the Latch-Key Killer: Profile of a Psychopath.'

Morgan was certainly confident about his diagnosis, she noted, looking up and muttering, 'thanks,' as Phil went out the door.

The volume was divided into two parts, one which examined the killings themselves and the police investigation to catch the murderer. The second was devoted to the trial and Morgan's interviews with Cummings whilst he was in Broadmoor. Dani decided she was more interested in the pattern of the man's crimes and the procedure used by the Met to catch Cummings than she was in some media-loving shrink's assessment of his motives.

Bevan flicked ahead to the first chapter and started to read.

Chapter 28

It was another hot day when Caitlin Hendry was led around Glasgow Green by Dr Lisa Fraser. The DC's research had brought her into contact with the academic, who was based at Clydebank University.

'There was a heatwave in the summer of 2005 as well, do you recall?'

'Not really, I was at school back then. I don't think I would have noticed,' the detective replied innocently.

Dr Fraser chuckled. 'Aye, you're not much older than my students, right enough.' She led her companion to the banks of the river, where they had a view across to the south Glasgow skyline, turned hazy by the heat. 'The fair started out as a place where folk could display and sell their cattle and livestock. The Green would have been full of animals during the event in the 19th Century, not bouncy castles and bumper cars like it is today. The farmers even came to these fairs to hire labourers. It must have been reminiscent of a slave auction at times.'

'When did the travelling fairgrounds become popular?'

'By the end of the 19th Century, amusements had triumphed over the agricultural element of the fair. At that point, the events were probably in their heyday, with illusionists and acrobats and even the first mechanical rides. When steam power came along, the rides became larger and more innovative. However, at the same time as the machinery was becoming more sophisticated, there was a movement growing against the 'showmen' who operated them. These itinerant communities were described in parliament as 'the dregs of society'.'

'Those attitudes are still around now.'

'Aye, certainly, and the hostility just made the so-called 'van-dwellers' more united and determined to preserve their way of life. The Showman's Guild was formed in 1917. It's still around today to protect the rights of fairground families.'

'Like a trade union.'

'Yes, exactly. But the real enemy of the travelling fairgrounds has been the redevelopment of their traditional pitches. As new housing is built in every piece of brownfield land surrounding the big cities, the travellers are squeezed out. Nobody wants to live near a travellers' settlement. That's the sad truth of it.'

Caitlin nodded. 'Do you know anything about the O'Driscoll family?'

'I'm afraid I haven't heard of them, but I suspect they were originally Irish immigrants who came over to Glasgow after the famine in the 1840s. Whether they were itinerant before that time it's impossible to tell.'

'Do many fairground families still operate in Scotland?'

'Yes, quite a few. You should contact the Guild for more details. Travelling children have been required to attend local schools since the 1880s. If the travelling family you're looking for has been dispersed then you'll probably find members of them still working as operators in the established fairgrounds. It's the work they've always known, one is reluctant to suggest it's in their blood, but many professions are, you know.' Dr Fraser smiled.

'My dad was a policeman.'

'There you go then, I rest my case.'

The young DC put out her hand. 'Thank you very much Dr Fraser, you've been a great help.'

Alice had driven them down the A77 to Ayr. The company they were looking for was based on an anonymous industrial estate on the outskirts of the town. The detectives had arranged to meet the managing director at the office building adjacent to a huge warehouse.

'Good morning, ladies.' the man greeted them with a broad smile. 'I'm Callum Reid, the MD of ScotRide.'

They took a seat. 'You know why we're here?' Alice began.

'You'd like a list of my employees. Yes, I received your e-mail. My HR assistant has printed off an Excel file.' Reid handed over a couple of sheets of paper.

Hendry skimmed through the names. 'These are your permanent staff?'

'Aye. I've got over fifty drivers and operators. They go out to events all over the country.' He crossed his thick arms over his chest. The action stretched his suit jacket to the limit. The seams were nearly bursting under the pressure.

'What about special occasions like the Glasgow Fair?' Hendry enquired. 'We had to bring officers in from other divisions. Didn't you need to call on extra staff?'

Reid frowned. 'I'm not sure if...,' the question had obviously unsettled him.

Alice bent forward, her expression steely. 'We don't care if you were paying folk cash in hand, or using illegals. We just need those names. A man was murdered that night. We think he may have hooked up with his killer on Glasgow Green earlier in the day. If we don't know exactly who was there, we can't eliminate your company from our inquiries. My boss will probably have to say as much on Crime

Scotland. I don't expect that publicity will be particularly welcome. People don't really like sending their kiddies out to fun parks operated by potential murderers.'

Callum Reid's face had drained of all colour. 'Come on officers, times are difficult enough as it is.' He pulled open a drawer beneath the desk. 'I never use illegals, let's get that straight. But there are a few men I call upon if I need extra hands. They're all good workers, with plenty of experience. I only use them occasionally, so we make a private arrangement. It's not illegal.'

'Just give me the names, Mr Reid. Every single one of them.'

Chapter 29

Rain was thundering down onto the empty pavements as Ryan Stone made his way along a back street in Notting Hill Gate. His flat was on the second floor of an attractive 1930s art deco block that was favoured by young, creative types.

Ryan was no exception. He worked for a small publishing company in Marble Arch. The apartment was bought when property prices in this area of London had been very reasonable. It was Holland Park and Bayswater that had possessed the most desirable postcodes back then. But now, the value of flats in the area was soaring beyond Ryan's wildest expectations.

He reached into his shoulder bag for the key, noticing the light on in the basement below, feeling a sense of relief that he wasn't living down there, below street level, where the new band of homeless types that had sprung up around the city in recent years had taken to urinating through the iron railings onto the owner's subterranean courtyard.

The stairwell was dark. The bulb at the top of the landing must have given out again. The management company were useless at dealing with that kind of thing. Ryan and his neighbours had taken to replacing it themselves and divvying out the smaller maintenance jobs between them. They were showing some initiative. Ryan smiled to himself, Mrs Thatcher would be proud. He knew she was going out of favour in a number of the circles he moved in but Ryan still liked the PM. He'd done pretty well out of her.

The flat was cold. Ryan reached across to notch up the heating. Half an hour's blast should warm the place up. He went straight into the kitchen and opened the fridge, ready to fix a quick supper so he could get on with the manuscript corrections he had to make by morning. Ryan laid out the ingredients for a simple omelette and strode into the bedroom, pulling off his shirt and trousers, reaching for the jogging pants and t-shirt he kept folded on the edge of the bed. Before he had a chance to put them on, he received a hard blow to the back of his head.

Ryan woke up maybe ten minutes later. His face felt itchy and weird. He tried to put a hand up to scratch it but found his wrists were tied down. The man wriggled about, discovering he was tethered to the radiator in the hallway. Then he winced, the metal pipes behind his bare back were burning hot. He attempted to pull himself away from the scalding surface but found it impossible to get free.

The itchiness was caused by the thick strip of masking tape that was wrapped around his mouth, the sharp edges rubbing at his skin. Ryan allowed his eyes to dart around the apartment. They rested on a tall, thin figure, standing absolutely still in the doorway to the lounge. There was something about this person's posture that he found familiar.

Ryan screwed his eyes tight shut as the figure approached his prostrate form, gritting his teeth against the pain which was already shooting across his back. The intruder let his hand slide along Ryan's naked thigh, which was wet with sweat and possibly blood too, from the head wound that Ryan could now feel as a dull, relentless throb. As the figure began to speak, in a croaky, almost childlike voice, his victim abruptly realised just exactly who this fiend was and cursed himself for his own damned stupidity.

Ryan Stone, 26, was the first of Ian Cummings' victims. He was murdered at his Notting Hill flat in March 1989. Stone's body was left on the floor of the hallway. No attempts having been made to remove the corpse or even try to cover it up. Morgan's interpretation of this was that there was no automatic sense of remorse from the perpetrator, as there usually was once the adrenaline of the killing had subsided. Cummings, he concluded, lacked the capacity to feel any sympathy towards the men he had butchered.

Dani was primarily interested in how the Met police had investigated this first crime. The use of DNA profiling was in its infancy. But it had been around for long enough to put criminals on their guard. Ian Cummings had used condoms during his assault on Stone and taken the soiled items away with him.

He'd worn gloves and a mask, meaning there was no transference of DNA or prints left in the flat. The perplexing aspect for the investigating officers was the fact that the killer had got into the property with ease. No signs of forced entry were evident.

Stone's immediate neighbours were all out at the time the murder took place. There was someone at home in the basement apartment but they claimed to have seen and heard nothing. Dani could see the SIO's problem. It wasn't really until the next victim turned up, three weeks later, that they could begin to discern a pattern.

After Alastair Whitlow's murder, at his flat in Shepherd's Bush, the police could start to identify a precedent. Whitlow was openly gay and was a prominent fundraiser for The Terence Higgins Trust. The victim had lost the man who'd been his first boyfriend to AIDS in 1987.

The Met were now pretty certain that the killer was targeting the homosexual community. They created a focus area for their search, a circle with a two mile radius around the murder sites. Usually, the area would have been larger, but they suspected that the killer was using the tube network to get about. Without the use of a car, they reduced his potential sphere of influence.

It was also concluded that the perpetrator must be known to the victims. He was obviously entering their flats with a key. This information was leaked to the press in early April 1989. Soon after, the first front page referring to the west London, 'Latch-Key Killer' appeared. Despite the Met officers being hostile to this nick-name, it was the press publicity that provided the team with their first proper break.

On the 24th April, a man entered Paddington police station claiming to have spent the night with the latch-key killer. Graham Clark was 21 years old and a student. His digs were in Ladbroke Grove. He'd met a young man he described as, 'very good looking' at a nightclub in the west end. They travelled back to Clark's shared house, but as the student showed the man in, he apparently became suddenly agitated. Clark was convinced that this was because he realised it was a communal property. They had sex in Clark's room, but the other man left early in the morning, before any of the housemates were up. He'd never heard from the guy again.

When Clark read about the murders in the newspaper, he became convinced that 'Tim', as he had called himself, was so unsettled that night because he'd expected the student to live alone. This would have given Tim the opportunity to return there at a later date to murder him. As it was, Clark's living arrangements didn't fit with what the killer wanted.

The police didn't set any great store by Clark's claims at first, but they recorded and filed his statement, including his detailed description of the man who had picked him up at the nightclub.

When murders three and four took place, still with no forensic traces left behind, the SIO was forced to return to Graham Clark's statement. One of the DIs suggested they establish a kind of sting operation. A young detective constable agreed to act as the 'bait'. DC Harry Kyle attended the same nightclub as Clark for three consecutive weekends. Finally, he spotted a man that fitted the description they had.

Kyle needed to tread carefully. From what Clark had told them, 'Tim' liked to approach the targets himself. The operation wouldn't work at all if the detective made the running. At the end of a long night, when Kyle was starting to think it was all in vain, Tim came to join him at the bar, casually enquiring if he would like a drink.

Chapter 30

The Met operation had a problem. Kyle needed to get Tim back to his Maida Vale flat and afford him the opportunity to make a copy of his key without actually having to have sex with him.

A scenario had been worked out ahead of time. After DC Kyle and Tim entered the flat, the detective went straight into the kitchenette to fix them both a drink. He called into the lounge that he was going to take a shower. Kyle allowed the man plenty of time to do what he had to.

At exactly 1.45am, the fire alarm for the entire building went off. Kyle insisted they troop out onto the pavement like the rest of the residents. As they'd hoped, Tim quickly made his excuses and headed off, clearly not wishing to be identifiable to the neighbours.

Plain-clothed officers followed Tim home to his dingy one-bedder in White City. They now had an address. It didn't take long to ascertain that 'Tim' was in fact Ian Cummings, 24 years old, currently unemployed, having spent a childhood in and out of children's homes and psychiatric institutions.

Cummings was now the Met's prime suspect. However, they possessed no solid evidence against him. All they could do from this point onwards was to place the man under surveillance and wait.

DC Kyle stuck to his cover. He was leaving the flat in the morning and travelling on the tube to Bond Street, where he worked a shift in one of the large department stores, returning at 6.30pm on the dot. After ten days of this routine and much debate within the division as to how likely the scheme was to ever get a result, Cummings struck.

The subsequent inquiry concluded that whilst he was in the flat with Kyle, the suspect must have unlocked the sash and case window leading from the rear fire escape to the lounge.

DC Kyle didn't know the layout of the property well and hadn't noticed this had been done. So when he arrived that day, Cummings entered the apartment from the back. The officers who were watching the place from the street, didn't know he was inside.

There'd been delays on the Central Line and Kyle himself was a little late getting home. His colleagues out front hadn't given him the signal, so Kyle went straight in. He wasn't on his guard at all. The young DC padded into the bedroom, taking off his shirt and pulling on a sweater. He'd not seen his girlfriend in a week and she was beginning to give him grief. DC Kyle made a move into the hallway, in order to give her a call from the landline.

This was the moment that Cummings attacked. He burst out of the bathroom, where he'd been hiding, and barged DC Kyle to the floor, attempting to strike his head with the metal ashtray he'd brought with him. Kyle twisted away, managing to deflect the blow. Cummings became increasingly angry, striking at Kyle repeatedly. But the DC succeeded in crawling along the smooth tiles to the bedroom, where he tugged his radio off the bed and switched it on. The support vehicle picked up the sound of the commotion, entering the flat within minutes and apprehending Cummings as he tore down the fire escape.

A search of Cummings' bedsit turned up the putty imprints that the killer had used to make copies of the keys to his victims' properties.

Cummings had an associate he'd known since childhood, who had a little side-line in key cutting. This man's home was also raided by the Met. The guy got five years.

With the evidence mounting up against him, Cummings decided to confess, using his history of psychiatric disorders as an explanation for his actions. This resulted in the murderer ending up in Broadmoor and was the reason for the campaign launched to agitate for his release in 2003. It failed. Cummings was still to this day serving an indefinite sentence of incarceration.

Detective Constable Harry Kyle suffered a severe concussion after the attack and although he received a medal for bravery, he didn't return to the police force. According to Morgan's book, Kyle and his girlfriend moved to her homeland of New Zealand in the 90s, where Harry took up private security work.

Ian Cummings had brutally murdered four young men and assaulted Harry Kyle in the space of two months. The case had sent shock waves out across the homosexual communities of London. Dani wasn't surprised that Phil's parents had been so worried about his brother. The events had cast a long shadow, with much of the conservative press commenting in their editorials on the promiscuous nature of the lives these young men had lived.

Morgan made much of the cultural reactions to the murders in his book, suggesting it changed the behaviour patterns of a generation of young gay men far more than the spectre of AIDS ever had.

Dani flicked through the section that dealt with Morgan's interviews with Cummings. She wasn't interested in all the psychobabble that no doubt accompanied the transcripts. It was the police investigation which intrigued the DCI. As she reviewed the first half of the book, Dani couldn't help but reflect that there was something about the west London murders case which left her feeling distinctly uneasy.

Chapter 31

It had been an hour now, since Andy Calder arrived at the smart, modern apartment block in Maryhill. It was already 7pm and the detective was beginning to wonder if the guy he was waiting for was ever going to return home.

Then he spotted a well-dressed man in his early fifties approaching along the leafy street. He was tall and lean, with his neatly cropped silver hair the only indication of his age. The man's stride shortened when he noticed Andy standing by the gate. For a moment, it looked as if he'd seen a ghost.

Calder stepped forward to introduce himself, before the man suffered a heart attack. 'Ben? It's Andy Calder, here. I don't know if you remember me?'

Ben Price put out his hand, his face creasing with relief. 'Of course I do. For a moment there I thought you were him – just walking up to me like I imagined for years he might do. Even though I know now that's not possible.'

'Sorry. I didn't mean to unsettle you.'

Price chuckled. 'It isn't your fault you look so much like Don. Please come inside.'

He led Andy up a wide staircase to his first floor flat. It was simply furnished with nicely chosen, clearly expensive objects. 'Coffee? Or something stronger?'

'What are you having?'

'Well, I usually pour myself a chilled glass of Sauvignon Blanc at this time of the day.' Ben pulled open the fridge, peering inside.

'That's what I'll have too then.'

They settled at the breakfast bar. Andy felt the man opposite seemed very relaxed in his presence. 'You don't appear particularly surprised to see me.'

Ben took a sip of wine. 'I know the police found Don's body. It was in the Herald. I've been half expecting someone to come and visit. I thought it might be Mae.'

'I'm a policeman now, a detective constable, although I'm on leave. My DCS won't let me anywhere near Don's case.'

The man smiled. 'But you're investigating it anyway.'

Andy chuckled. 'Something like that.' He shifted his weight on the stool. 'Mae told me that at one time you and Don had been more than just friends.'

'Ah, I wondered when that was going to come out. I wanted to inform the police about his sexuality when Don went missing, but Mae asked me not to. I don't know why I listened to her, really. My loyalty should have been to Don. But she said it would stain his memory, which is actually hugely insulting.'

'When did you and Don have a relationship?'

'Oh, it was decades ago. Mid-eighties, perhaps? I always knew that Donny liked girls too. There was no point in my falling head over heels in love with him. It was obvious he'd get married someday. So I always held myself back. That's why we were able to remain friends.'

'Mae believes that Don was battling with his sexuality in the months before he went missing. Did he ever speak with you about it?'

Ben shook his head sadly. 'We weren't as close by then as we'd once been. I only wish he had. When Don was living the hetero family dream, it would have been awkward to have me popping round every five minutes. Although, I did receive a phone call from him, maybe a month before the Glasgow Fair.'

'What did he say?' Andy shifted up with interest.

Ben sighed. 'It was a melancholy conversation. Don was a bit tipsy and reminiscing about the past. We'd had some great times together. He was certainly very sad about something. He talked about discovering that people you'd once respected were just pawns of the system, out for profit and their own ends. It was the kind of stuff Don would have railed on about when we were still young. It made me sure that Don had taken his own life when he disappeared.'

'But he didn't. Someone killed him.' Andy finished his wine. 'If Don was tempted to start seeing men again, how would he go about it? Were there any particular bars or clubs you used to frequent?'

His host looked thoughtful. 'I can give you a list of a few. It's amazing how many of these places are still going strong and are quite unchanged from how they were twenty five years ago.' He smiled, 'which is more than can be said for the clientele.'

Andy glanced around him. 'Are you married now?'

'To a man, you mean? No. I had a partner for a long time but he died last year. I don't expect there will be anyone else for me.'

'I'm very sorry.'

Ben nodded in recognition. Then he tilted his head to one side. 'You aren't at all like Don described you.'

'How do you mean?' Andy felt his stomach flip over.

'Well, it was you and your father that had kept Donny in the closet for all those years. He thought the Calders would disown him if they ever knew. Yet here you are, casually asking me if I'm married to another man.'

Andy shrugged his shoulders. 'People change,

they have to.'

'What about your father, has he changed his opinions too?'

Calder didn't answer, but the sad expression on his face told Ben Price all he needed to know.

*

Andy left Price's flat with plenty of time to drop into a few of the bars on the list. Carol knew he might be home late. On this occasion, Andy hadn't needed to lie to her.

Calder was required to shrug off his prejudices and stroll confidently through the area of the west-end where the gay establishments proliferated. The places that Ben and Don used to frequent were less glitzy than many of the others. Andy felt they were just like any other trendy pub, except the clientele were predominantly male. He bought a bottle of lager at a place called the Lime Tree and positioned himself on a stool at the bar.

The evening cabaret was about to start. It constituted a half decent rock band performing their set in full make-up and wigs. Calder thought it was very reminiscent of 70s glam rock. He'd found the music pretty good. Andy also noted how he'd been propped up at the bar for an hour at least and not one man had approached him. This fact shattered another myth that most straight men held about drinking in a gay bar. These guys weren't interested in him at all.

Andy wasn't entirely sure what he was doing here, after all these years had passed. There wasn't going to be anyone still hanging around who remembered Don from the day he went missing. He supposed it was more like he was trying to get into the head of his uncle. Andy had needed to completely shift the perception he'd had of a man he'd loved most of his life. This trip was part of the process.

He was about to move onto the next establishment on the list when Andy noticed a lad standing with a group at the other side of the bar. He was in his twenties, wearing a tightly fitting bright green t-shirt and with his blond hair gelled into a messy, bed-head type of style. Sensing someone staring at him, the young man looked over, his face freezing in shock when he recognised Calder.

Andy raised his hand in a friendly gesture. He made his way slowly through the crowd, intent upon buying DC Dan Clifton a drink.

Chapter 32

'What are you doing here? If you don't mind me asking.' Dan had broken away from his pals and led Andy towards a quieter table by the window.

'I've found out that my uncle Don spent quite a bit of his time in here, when he was a younger man. I suppose I thought it might give me some kind of insight into his state of mind.'

'What it's like to be gay, you mean?' Dan sipped from a tumbler filled with an orange coloured concoction.

'Yeah, that's probably what I mean.'

'This is one aspect of the lifestyle, sure. But we don't get many guys in here over forty.'

Andy's face crinkled in a grin. 'Point taken.'

'Look,' Dan fiddled with the beer mat. 'I'm not out at work. I kinda want to keep it that way.'

'I'm not going to say anything. But can I ask why? Things are different these days. DCI Bevan would never hold it against you for a start.'

'Oh, it's not her. Alice and Phil would be cool, too.' Dan looked suddenly uneasy. 'It's the other guys – the uniforms and the DCs. You've heard the brand of jokes they tell. Not in front of Bevan, sure. But you and I know exactly what their opinions are.'

'I've told some of those sorts of jokes myself.' Andy sipped his beer, feeling awkward.

'Yeah and I never expected in a million years to see you in a place like this. I don't think there's anyone at Pitt Street who's more overtly hetero than you are. If a lassie possesses anything less than a

34" chest she's not even on your radar.'

'Is that really how I come across?' Andy cradled the ice cold bottle in his hands.

Dan chuckled. 'Yes, it is. But the DCI loves you down to your un-PC little toes. So that's okay.'

Andy felt uncomfortable. It wasn't easy being presented so starkly with how the rest of the world viewed you.

'Don't look so worried, man. It's only really Alice and me who see things that way. The rest of the division think you're a standard bearer for common sense on the force. It just depends which side of the fence you're on.'

'What if my position is starting to shift?'

Dan leant forward and patted him on the back, emboldened by the lethal cocktail he'd been merrily supping for the past hour. 'Well, if that's really the case DC Calder, it would amount to a sodding revolution.'

*

DC Clifton was dressed more formally as he attended DCI Bevan's briefing the following morning, his hangover carefully masked by a hot shower and a decent moisturiser. Alice and Caitlin were presenting the evidence they'd gathered. Dan could sense some of the older men stiffening at the sight of all these women steering the course of the investigation. No one would say anything of course, it was just a feeling he got.

'We've got a set of names from ScotRide,' Alice continued, handing out sheets to the group. 'They all need to be checked out. Caitlin and I have already started. We're trying to create a background profile on them all.'

'So, we want to ascertain if any of the men

working the Glasgow Fair this year have a link to the now defunct 'Coco's' operation which provided the amusements ten years ago,' Bevan clarified.

Clifton put up his hand. 'I've been looking into the Donny Calder case, Ma'am. I had a conversation with an ex-boyfriend of his who's given me a list of their old haunts. Maybe Calder visited one of them on the day he went missing. If he was feeling nostalgic about his past life before he was married, he may just have decided to take a trip down memory lane.' It wasn't Dan's idea to take the credit for this. Andy had insisted that the information was investigated properly, making the young DC promise he'd put it forward.

Bevan looked surprised. 'Well done. Get someone else on board and look into it further, would you?'

Dan nodded.

The DCI turned to address the room. 'We've got plenty to do. I realise we've not got many red-hot leads, but it's going to be solid, plodding police work that gets this guy caught. I really don't want us to have another murder on our hands before we can stop him in his tracks.'

Chapter 33

He'd never spotted the guy in the Lime Tree before. He was certainly good-looking, in a rugged, care-worn kind of way. But what he'd noticed immediately was the wedding ring. These days, you couldn't be too sure if it represented one of those civil partnership things. In the case of this guy, the gold band was too well-worn, fitted too neatly into the folds of skin which enveloped it. This man had got hitched at least a decade ago. Which meant his partner must be a woman.

After an hour, he approached a younger man by the bar. He bought him a drink and led him off to a private table, away from the crowds. But they didn't go home together. The older guy left the place first. It was easy enough to follow him. He caught the bus from Cowcaddens and got off along the Great Western Road, entering the door of a low rise block of flats. The address was quickly noted before the observer put his head down and his hood up, proceeding back to the main road, where he would easily be able get a bus home himself.

*

Phil Boag approached his boss's office, knocking urgently, an optimistic look on his face.

'What is it?' Bevan shifted up in her seat.

'We've had a call in response to the Crime Scotland piece we did, someone who claims to have recognised that ring. Not Donny Calder's one but that little gold signet.'

Dani jumped to her feet. 'Are they still on the line?'

'No, he had to go. Palmer took a name and address, but not until he jotted down the man's story.'

'Brilliant. Let's pay him a visit.'

'Err, that might be tricky. He lives in Vancouver. The guy only just watched the Crime Scotland programme on the BBC satellite channel. That's why it's taken him so long to respond to the appeal.'

Bevan sat down again with a bump. 'Right. Get me the number. I'll give him a call.'

Spencer McAuliffe had been based in Canada for eight years. He worked for an international bank. He told Bevan how he returned to Glasgow every few years, but since having children, they made the journey less often. McAuliffe was now in his mid-thirties but back in the 90s he'd attended a private school near to his parents' home in Wemyss Bay.

Spencer was convinced that the signet ring he saw nestled amongst the other items on Crime Scotland was once owned by an old science master at his school. He claimed to remember it because the teacher had often used it as a part of his experiments, dangling the ring on the end of a piece of string and that sort of thing. He had recalled Mr Ross so clearly because of what had become of him.

Douglas Ross had been swept into the sea during a coastal walk in 1997. McAuliffe described how the entire school were in mourning for weeks. He had been a much loved teacher and assistant housemaster. Spencer had been a sixth-former back then so it was very strongly imprinted upon his memory. He speculated as to whether the ring had got washed up onto a shore somewhere and somebody had found it, the item then turning up all these decades later amongst the random detritus in that plastic bag.

Bevan thanked McAuliffe very much for his information, promising to keep him updated on any results. As she set down the receiver, the DCI felt sure that this tip off was a sound one. Bevan had learnt early on in her career that sometimes it just took one person who observed the minutiae of life more than the average to provide that elusive connection which cracked a case. The timing of Spencer's account certainly seemed to fit. The wrist watch was dated by their experts as having originated from the early nineties, when the model was widely available throughout the UK. Dani wondered if the watch had been Ross's too. She tried to contain her excitement. This was a fresh lead. They had a new name to work from. The DCI swiftly called together her team. They didn't have a moment to lose.

Chapter 34

Douglas Ross was 46 years old in 1997. He had a wife and two children, both of them of university age at the time he disappeared. His wife passed away less than a decade after her husband was pronounced missing, presumed dead. She was only in her early fifties.

Ross had been a senior schoolmaster at Wemyss College for the majority of his career. The witnesses who spoke at the inquest into his death paid tribute to his dedication as a teacher to the many boys he'd come into contact with over the years.

It was during the spring break of 1997 when Ross informed his wife that he was going to spend the day searching for fossils and precious stones down on the shore at Wemyss Bay. Ross was an amateur geologist in his spare time. He often scoured the beaches for the garnets and amethysts which were thrown up by the ancient Highland Fault line and then washed up on the banks of the Clyde.

A witness had seen him descending the coastal path at Wemyss Bay in the late morning. Then a dog-walker was sure she'd spotted a man matching Ross's description on the beach itself, to the north of the Pier. They exchanged pleasantries before the woman returned to the town.

It was the end of March and the week in which the Clyde experienced its Spring tide. The locals had noticed how fast the water had come into the shore that day. The sharp southerly wind made the waves tall and strong. Ross never returned home that evening.

His wife called the police and the coastal rescue

service. They searched the beach and cliffs until daybreak. No sign of the man was found. It was decided at the inquest that Ross had become preoccupied with his hunt for fossils, enthusiastic as he was about his hobby. The tide had rushed upon him unexpectedly, sweeping him out into the powerful currents of the Clyde.

A body was never recovered, but the Procurator Fiscal was satisfied that enough evidence pointed to the fact it was death by misadventure. This was the official verdict that was reached.

'So Mr Ross didn't turn up in any of the searches we performed for missing persons reported in the Glasgow area in the 90s and 2000s. He wasn't officially missing. The man had been declared dead,' Alice Mann explained, after having spent the morning examining the findings of the inquest.

'Do you think he was really swept out to sea?' The DCI directed her steady gaze at the detective constable.

Alice screwed up her face. 'The witnesses were a bit flaky, Ma'am, especially the dog walker who claimed to have seen Ross on the beach. This woman didn't actually know Mr Ross but had assumed it was him after watching a reconstruction on the local news. I wouldn't have treated her testimony as particularly reliable.'

'I suppose it was simply the most likely conclusion based on the evidence they had,' Phil added. 'Everyone assumed that Douglas Ross had done exactly what he told his wife he was going to do. But with that ring turning up in the same bag as the trophies from Calder and McLaren, it puts a whole new complexion on the incident.'

Bevan nodded sombrely. 'We need to tread carefully on this. The first thing I propose we do is to organise a meeting with Ross's children. I need a proper identification of the signet ring before we start spreading the idea that this well-regarded teacher and family man was taken by some kind of psychotic serial killer.'

A ripple of agreement echoed around the room.

*

Beverley Williams lived with her family in Helensburgh. She worked as a legal secretary in a solicitor's office in the town and had arranged to come home early so she could receive the detectives.

Alice and Dan approached the property and rang the bell. The house was a dormer bungalow with a pretty garden encircling it, just on the right side of being overgrown. Alice pricked her finger on one of the rose bushes snaking up the wall next to the front door. As Beverley led them inside, the officer had the digit lodged firmly in her mouth, sucking up the blood.

'Would you like a plaster?' The woman asked. 'My husband keeps meaning to cut that bush back. He hasn't quite got round to it yet.'

'No thank you, Mrs Williams. It'll stop bleeding in a minute.'

Alice knew that Beverley was in her late thirties but she looked older, imagining it must be her old fashioned high collared blouse and knee length chequered skirt which gave that impression. 'Are your children at home?'

She shook her head of short, wavy hair. 'I've asked a friend to pick them up from school. I assumed it wouldn't be wise to have them here.'

'That was a good idea.'

Beverley led them into a small lounge, facing out onto a long thin garden. 'I'll put the kettle on.'

The detectives allowed her to perform this ritual, knowing that keeping people busy always helped in these situations. She brought in a tray a few minutes later. 'Now, I assume this is all about Dad.'

Dan edged forward on the floral sofa, the evidence bag bulging in his pocket. 'We need to see if you recognise an object, Mrs Williams. We have reason to believe it may have belonged to your father.'

The woman slipped on a pair of small rimmed glasses that were resting on the coffee table, another action which prematurely aged her. 'Come on then, let's have a look.'

Dan fished into his pocket and brought out the plastic pouch. He slid the gold ring into the palm of his hand. To their great surprise, Beverley smiled.

'Can I touch it?'

'Of course.' Dan handed it over.

She positioned it between her thumb and forefinger, holding it up to the light. 'It's definitely Dad's. It was what he used to call his play ring. He wore it on his little finger, but was always working it off. My father performed a trick where he pretended that the ring had disappeared behind our ears and then he produced it again. Like folk do with coins.'

Dan nodded.

'Where did you find it?' Beverley gazed at her lap, obviously frightened of the answer.

'Have you heard about the McLaren case down in Giffnock?' Alice placed her hand on the woman's arm.

She raised her head abruptly. 'Yes, but what...?' A hand sprung up to cover her mouth, her expression one of horror.

'A bag was found near to the place where Mr McLaren's body was recovered. It contained a number of items, some of them belonging to the man who was killed and others that had been the property of men who'd gone missing from the Glasgow area in the last fifteen years, their whereabouts having never been properly determined.'

A flash of hope passed across Beverley's face. 'Well, that rules Dad out. He had an accident. It was awful but just one of those things. He was collecting precious stones out at Wemyss Bay. The strong tide washed him into the water. The currents took his body as far away as the Atlantic Ocean they thought. That's why I like to live by the water myself. It makes me feel closer to him.'

Alice cleared her throat. 'With your father's ring being amongst these items, we believe that the findings of the inquiry into your father's death may have been incorrect. It might be possible he was never on that beach at all on the day he went missing.'

Beverley's eyes filled with tears. 'Then what *was* he doing – where is he now?'

'That is what we intend to find out, Mrs Williams.' Alice placed her arm around the woman's shoulders, squeezing gently, suddenly quite certain that whatever they did discover about the fate of her father, it wasn't going to make the poor lady feel any better.

Then the detective looked down, noticing that a drip of blood from her pricked finger had seeped onto the sleeve of Beverley's white cotton blouse, creating a deep crimson stain which was unlikely to ever come out.

Chapter 35

'I think we can now be confident that there are at least three victims.' Dani stood to face her officers. 'The first murder that we're aware of was in 1997, followed by Donald Calder in 2005, and then Nathan McLaren in 2015.'

Phil's brow furrowed deeply. 'We had a connection when both the victims had visited the Glasgow Fair on the day they went missing. With Douglas Ross added to the equation, we lose that unifying factor.'

DC Caitlin Hendry put up her hand. 'Perhaps the link has nothing to do with the Glasgow Fair specifically.'

'Go on,' Dani urged.

Hendry looked thoughtful. 'Alice and I have been investigating the people who provided the entertainments on the Glasgow Green that Saturday. Perhaps we don't need to focus on the weekend itself, but on the travelling fairground. The whole point of it is that the show isn't tied to one particular location.'

Bevan straightened her posture. 'Isn't there a big caravan park at Wemyss Bay?'

'It's a holiday park,' Phil answered. 'We took the girls there a few times when they were little.'

'Isn't that the type of place where a fairground would set itself up, especially during school holidays?' Bevan glanced around the group, registering the nods and grunts of her officers. 'Caitlin, can you and Alice check that out for me? I want to know every single recreational activity that went on in the Wemyss Bay area during the spring break of 1997.'

*

Calder loitered by the main gate that led to St Columba's Park. He recalled how much time he'd spent on the terraces as a lad with his father and Don. For the first time, the idea struck Andy that he'd never have a son; that this Calder ritual wouldn't be played out again in his generation. Then he stopped himself short. He imagined DCI Bevan informing him, in no uncertain terms, that there was nothing preventing him from bringing Amy along on a Saturday afternoon.

The detective was just considering whether he had time to nip into the shop and buy her one of the kiddie-sized kits when the man he was waiting for emerged from the building beyond. He opened a door in the gate for Calder to pass through.

'Hi Terry,' he said, shaking his hand. 'It's been a very long time.'

'Aye, it certainly has.' Terry Finch led Andy down a corridor lined with team photos, pausing when he reached his office. 'Take a seat. I've a bottle of single malt in the drawer.'

Calder shook his head with a sigh. 'No thanks, Pal. I've got the car outside.' He didn't actually say he was on duty, but this was the impression Andy was hoping to give.

'No problem, I understand. Now, what is it I can help you with?' Terry poured himself out a wee dram, relaxing back into his seat and holding the glass to his lips like a microphone.

'Did you hear we found Uncle Don's body?'

Terry frowned. 'Aye. I'm very sorry for you all. How's Mae bearing up?'

'He'd been gone a long time. Mae was pretty sure

he was dead. She's relieved to be able to lay him to rest.'

Terry nodded sagely. 'I can see that. But it's tough, all the same. She loved him to pieces. That fact was obvious to us all.'

'You know the book he was writing about the club? Mae thinks that Don came to see you to discuss it in the week before he disappeared. Do you recall what you talked about?'

'It was a decade ago, Andy. I'm not sure I can really help.'

'Did the police come here after Don went missing? Were you ever questioned about meeting him?'

The man made a face. 'Not that I remember. Don met with me a lot during that period. I honestly couldn't tell you the dates. Your uncle was making really great progress with his research. I was hoping to get a first draft by the end of that summer.' Terry took a sip of whisky.

Andy cleared his throat. 'How well did you know Don back then – were you close enough for him to confide in you?'

'I'd commissioned his book, but we were also friends. I knew that Don had his demons. He told me that sometimes he got really low. For what it's worth, I always thought that perhaps Mae wasn't the right lassie for him. He never spoke about her the way I used to speak about Val. I can't really explain what I mean by that. There was just a lack of warmth in his tone, I suppose. It was evident when he talked about the kids, though.'

Andy nodded. He recognised what Finch was describing. When a man had fallen out of love with his wife, he usually had real trouble hiding it. A woman, on the other hand, could cover it up indefinitely. Calder stood up to leave. 'By the way, did you ever get hold of the manuscript?'

Terry looked puzzled. 'The stuff Don had written up to the point he disappeared, you mean?'

'Aye. You could have brought in another author to complete it, after all the work that had been done.'

Terry downed the rest of his drink. 'I never set eyes on that document and I wouldn't have wanted to. Don was like a little kid with that book. I was waiting for him to come back and finish the thing himself.'

Andy smiled, leaning forward to give the man a warm hug. 'Don would have appreciated that Terry, I'm certain of it.'

Chapter 36

When the weather was warm like this, Carol usually took Amy to the local park. Even with all the windows wide open, the flat got really hot in summer. Andy assumed that was where the girls would be, when he got home later that day to find the place empty.

He took the opportunity to remove the little football shirt and shorts from their plastic bag, laying the outfit on the kitchen table. The striking purple and white colours of the strip unlocked a sudden rush of memories. Andy had to blink feverishly to hold back the tide.

The front door opened out in the hall. With that sixth sense that toddlers seemed to possess when it came to presents, Amy ran into the kitchen and jumped up on a chair. 'Are they for me?' She cried.

'Of course, sweetheart. Do you want to try them on?'

The little girl grabbed the garments off the table and headed straight for her bedroom.

Carol made a beeline for the kettle instead. 'Do you want a coffee?'

'Aye, that would be great. How was the park – any other mums there?'

She turned, resting her weight on the counter. 'We had to come back early. One of the residents who lives across the street had called the police. She saw a man hanging around the playground.'

Andy's posture stiffened. 'Did he approach any of the kiddies?'

Carol shook her head, but she looked unsettled. 'I'd spotted him too. It was a hot day but he had the hood of his tracksuit top pulled up over his head. But then plenty of folk do that. I don't think I would have rung the bobbies.'

'Were you still there when the police arrived?'

'Aye, they'd sent a couple of uniformed officers. I didn't recognise either of them. By this point, the man had wandered off into the housing estate. They asked all the mums for a description. To be honest, I really didn't get a good look at his face.'

Andy stepped forward and placed his arms around her. 'You seem a bit rattled. Are you worried about Amy?'

Carol tipped her head back to catch his eye. 'The women were all blethering on about paedophiles and kiddie snatchers.' She paused. 'This is going to sound weird, but I had the funniest sensation that the man was actually watching *me*.'

Andy held her closer. He didn't get the chance to ask his wife any more about the man loitering at the playground. Amy bounded into the room behind him, spinning in circles and waving her arms in the air, the pristine football kit snuggly fitting her tiny form.

'Oh, you look gorgeous!' Carol exclaimed, removing herself from Andy's embrace and rushing off to find her camera.

*

Alice Mann was examining a map of the Firth of Clyde. Her own parents lived in Largs. They took a drive along the coast to Wemyss Bay occasionally, if Alice was over for Sunday lunch.

Wemyss Bay was probably best known as a port, where you could catch the ferry to the Isle of Bute. These days, Alice noted how the village was dominated by the huge caravan park, which no doubt brought a certain amount of tourism and wealth to the area. Alice's father had always been interested in trains. She recalled him waxing lyrical about the train station at Wemyss Bay, which he described as one of the finest railway buildings in Scotland. This meant that like Paisley and Giffnock, there was a reliable train service into the city of Glasgow.

The detective had already contacted the holiday park, who had no record of entertainments put on in the village back in 1997. The manager told her they had their own acts and cabaret at the park. They wouldn't have brought in outside contractors. He very helpfully sent over a list of the acts they were using back then, when they had far less amenities than they did now.

Caitlin Hendry approached Alice's desk. She gazed down at the map. 'From what I learnt about the Glasgow Fair from Dr Fraser, Wemyss Bay seems like the typical seaside resort that city folk would stream to during the Fair weekend. Hundreds of holidaymakers would line the piers along that strip of the coast, waiting for the steamers to take them to Rothesay or Brodick.'

'But I can't find any evidence of our travelling fairground having visited there.' Alice sighed.

'It was a long time ago,' Caitlin muttered. 'If they arrived and set up camp on one of the fields, I don't expect many folk would remember it now. No one pays much attention to the travelling fair. They stay for a week or so and then move on.'

'Have *you* had any luck?'

'I've been on the phone to the receptionist at Wemyss College. She was very helpful. They have extensive contacts within their alumni community, so 1997 didn't seem that long ago to them. The lady made us an appointment with the current deputy head. He knew Douglas Ross quite well.'

'Excellent. Then if the boss agrees, I suggest we concentrate for now on trying to find out everything we possibly can about our victim.'

Chapter 37

Wemyss College enjoyed an impressive position on a hillside just beyond the village. The grounds boasted a great view onto the Firth of Clyde and beyond it to the hills of Bute and Cumbrae.

The main school building was based in a formidably large stone house. Alice might even have gone as far as to describe it as a castle. The reception desk was positioned in a room off a wide entrance hall, where a grand staircase dominated the space.

Dr Kennedy's office was on the first floor. Caitlin glanced about her at the stags' heads that lined the walls. She found the formal atmosphere of the place faintly creepy. They discovered the door open and the deputy head standing by the window, staring out at the iron grey sea. He turned as the detectives entered.

'Please take a seat at my desk,' he commanded. Malcolm Kennedy was in his late fifties, tall and broad. His blue eyes twinkled as he smiled. 'I wasn't gazing out of the window and daydreaming, like a fifth former in double science on a Friday afternoon. I was actually thinking about Douglas, which I hadn't done in many years, much to my shame.'

'Did you know Mr Ross very well when he taught here?' Alice flipped open her pad.

'Douglas was already at Wemyss when I joined the school to teach Classics in '92. We must have been colleagues for five years at least before his disappearance. I met his wife at staff dinners on a number of occasions, she was a lovely woman. I believe the school did right by her and the children after Douglas was declared dead, although I wasn't management back then and wouldn't have been party to the details.'

'What was Mr Ross like? His wife is no longer around to tell us and the children don't always know, do they?'

Kennedy nodded. 'Quite true. Most people present only their best side to their offspring - or their worst, depending upon one's parenting style.' The man was obviously amused by his own observation. 'Douglas was the last of a certain breed of teacher.'

Caitlin looked puzzled.

'He was a maverick,' Kennedy continued. 'Douglas liked to joke with his classes and encouraged them to think outside the rules and regulations of this fine institution. The headmaster back then thought he was a subversive, but actually, Doug possessed a razor sharp intellect. His classes always sailed through their exams. He had the highest uptake of Oxbridge students.' He tapped his forehead. 'The man actually taught the boys how to reason for themselves.'

'So you can't imagine why anyone would have wanted to kill Mr Ross?' Alice leaned in.

Both detectives noticed a shadow pass across Kennedy's face. 'He was a highly valued member of staff. The school had absolute faith in his abilities.'

Alice wondered why the man had now reverted to soundbites when he'd previous been so candid.

'We don't have any desire to ruin Mr Ross's reputation, or bring your school any trouble,' Caitlin Hendry added tentatively. 'But we really need you to help us out a bit here. The evidence tells us that Douglas Ross found himself in the clutches of a very violent, ruthless person, yet this all happened nearly twenty years ago. His wife is dead and his children barely remember him. Can't you give us anything at all?'

Kennedy glanced at the young woman's plaintive expression and sighed. 'We are a small school here at Wemyss and have a strong community. The benefits of this are obvious, but there are some drawbacks. The boys have a tremendous knack of seeing into one's soul. Their minds are young and sharp, their instincts honed. Added to this, staff and pupils spend a great deal of time together.'

'What are you saying?' Alice was becoming impatient.

'I'm saying, detective constable, that there were rumours about Douglas Ross when he was a teacher here; barely formed whispers that passed between the boys in their dorms at night.'

'And what exactly did these rumours suggest about Mr Ross?'

Kennedy cleared his throat. 'That although Douglas was married, he was in true fact a homosexual.'

Chapter 38

'Well, we'd already guessed as much,' DCI Bevan commented, as Mann and Hendry stood in her office. 'How did the boys pick up on it? Was there any suggestion of Ross acting inappropriately towards them?'

'No Ma'am. The deputy head thought the boys just noticed him looking at the older lads a bit longer than he should. It was subtle stuff that's tricky to put your finger on and of course, it's hardly an offence to be a homosexual.'

'But not a great reputation to have if you are married,' Bevan added. 'So, do we think that Ross had a rendezvous with the man that killed him?'

'It's looking that way,' Alice replied. 'They must have come into contact with each other locally. The police records from back then suggested that Ross hadn't left Wemyss Bay for weeks before he set off on his supposed walk. It had been a busy term at the school, which had lessons on Saturday mornings in those days.'

'At least it limits the possibilities.'

Dan Clifton approached the door and knocked. 'I may have found something important, Ma'am,' he announced, before even stepping inside. 'I was speaking to the Admissions Officer at Wemyss College. She was providing me with the names of a few of Mr Ross's students, now alumni of the school. One of them was called Anthony Lomond, 31 years old, now living in Glasgow.'

Alice flinched. 'Tony? Did he go to Wemyss College? I knew his parents were from the Firth of Clyde somewhere. I didn't make the connection.'

'Check it out, please,' Bevan commanded. 'Then bring Mr Lomond back in here for a wee chat.'

*

Tony Lomond looked uncomfortable. He'd cultivated the beginnings of a stubbly beard since DC Mann had last seen him. Alice knew that her boss was monitoring the interview from the video room upstairs. Dan Clifton was sitting impassively beside her with the duty solicitor opposite him.

Alice was determined to take the lead. She pushed a large photograph across the desk towards Lomond. 'Do you recognise any of the items in that picture?'

He examined the image closely. 'No.'

The DC took it back, holding the photo up. 'These items were discovered not far from where Nathan McLaren's body was dumped. Some of the things here belonged to him.' Alice tapped the glossy image. 'This signet ring has also been identified. It was once the property of a Mr Douglas Ross, one time teacher at Wemyss College, Renfrewshire.'

Tony winced. Alice eyed him closely, noting the beads of sweat that had broken out across his forehead. 'How can that be possible?'

'Do you admit to knowing Mr Ross?'

'Of course, he was my science teacher at school.' The man dipped his head. 'I really liked him.'

'Were you aware that Douglas Ross was declared dead in April 1997 after an Inquest decided he'd been swept away by the tide at Wemyss Bay?'

He nodded. 'I was in third form when it happened. The staff and students were devastated. I cried when my tutor told me. I found it tough at school. I wasn't quite the same as the other boys, but Mr Ross was kind and sensitive, he appeared to understand. It was a tragedy that something like that had happened to him. He had children too, I recall.'

Alice knew that Lomond was thirteen years old when Ross disappeared. It seemed extremely unlikely that he could have been responsible for it. Yet this link between him and two of the victims was impossible to ignore. 'We believe now that Mr Ross may have been abducted by the same person who killed Nathan McLaren. How do you explain the fact that both of these men were known to you? It's an incredible coincidence, don't you think?'

Tony lifted his head and looked her in the eye. 'Actually, I'm not so sure it is.' He laid his hands flat on the table between them. 'The truth is that I *didn't* really know Nathan McLaren. I'd spoken to him a few times in bars, on the gay scene. It's actually quite a small world in Glasgow. I couldn't have told you anything more about him other than he drank Czech lager.' Tony shifted his gaze towards Dan. 'Take this officer, for instance. I've seen him several times in the Lime Tree with his mates. I might even have spoken to him on occasion. Does that mean your fellow DC *also* has a connection to these crimes?'

Dan Clifton's face had flushed to a deep pink. The Duty Solicitor noisily cleared her throat. Alice was shocked, but determined not to let it put her off her stride.

'I see what you're saying, Mr Lomond. But we only have your word that you didn't know Nathan McLaren better than that.'

Tony shrugged. 'My word is all I can offer you. Before I started the rowing I was a weedy little boy who was bullied by the bigger lads. The idea that at thirteen years of age I could have overpowered a grown man is simply preposterous.'

'My client has a point,' the solicitor chipped in. 'Mr Lomond has been extremely cooperative since the very start of this investigation. This *coincidence* you've uncovered doesn't really amount to much. I would also suggest that if one of your officers is known socially to my client and potentially to one of the victims, too, then he should be immediately removed from the case. If Mr Lomond is ever charged with these murders, I will have a duty to pass this information on to the defence team. It won't go down well in court.'

Alice blinked rapidly, sensing her colleague's body stiffen. 'Okay, Tony, that's all for now, you're free to go home. But be assured that we will need to speak with you again.'

Chapter 39

Bevan was standing by the filing cabinet whilst DC Dan Clifton was perched on the tiny sofa in her office. She realised her stance was intimidating but she really didn't feel like sitting down.

'Why the hell didn't you tell me you knew Tony Lomond socially?'

'I don't, Ma'am. He must have seen me out in some of the bars. I honestly don't recall speaking with him. I would have informed you if I had.'

'I hope you realise, that I have no problem whatsoever with you being gay. But you visiting the same bars as Lomond and McLaren has a *direct* bearing on my case. You should have told me immediately, DC Clifton. This information has placed me in an impossible position.'

Dan made his tone as strident as he could manage in the circumstances. 'I'm very sorry, Ma'am. I'm so used to keeping my sexuality a secret at work that it never crossed my mind to inform anyone. I swear I did not know Nathan McLaren. I'd never seen him before. Tony Lomond hasn't ever approached me in a bar, either. I believe that Lomond recognised me from the Glasgow scene and then decided to use that information as leverage in the interview.'

Bevan thought about this. 'Well, it certainly worked.'

'I can see how you might want me to steer clear of the McLaren side of the investigation. But why don't you let me work with Caitlin on the Ross case instead?' He gazed pleadingly at her.

'The DCS hasn't actually granted me the budget

to link the two crimes into a multiple murder hunt yet, so I don't see why not. I have no intention of allowing Tony Lomond to manipulate my choice of team'

'Thank you, Ma'am.' Clifton beamed. 'You won't regret it.'

*

Alice Mann was mightily pissed off. She was a little upset that Dan hadn't felt he could tell her that he was gay, especially with all the issues that had been raised by the McLaren case. But it wasn't him she was angry with, it was Lomond. The guy had deliberately set out to make them look like idiots; using Dan's sexuality to wriggle his way out of some awkward questions. He'd not hesitated in outing him to his colleagues. Talk about solidarity. Bastard.

She stared hard at the screen. Alice was determined to dig up everything there was to know about Anthony Elliot Lomond.

Lomond's parents, Michael and Rosemary, lived in Inverkip, a couple of miles from Wemyss Bay. Tony's father was now retired, having at one time been a manager at a shipyard in Port Glasgow. His mother was a housewife. They were both now in their late sixties. Michael Lomond had received three points on his licence the previous year for speeding on the A78. There were no other convictions recorded for the pair.

Alice considered Tony's background. Like her, he was an only child with slightly older parents. Alice's mum and dad lived further down the coast from Wemyss Bay in Largs. The DC could imagine why Tony hadn't yet told his family he was gay. Her own parents had always seemed strangely old-fashioned and at one remove from the social changes that had taken place in the modern world over the past thirty years.

Tony had attended the prep school at Wemyss College and remained there all the way through his schooling, until leaving for the University of Aberdeen to study Environmental Sciences in 2002. Alice assumed this was when he took up the rowing. According to Lomond himself, before that point he'd been a small, weedy adolescent. Tony didn't become a fully grown adult for another five years after Douglas Ross's disappearance.

She studied the map of Renfrewshire closely. There were two small reservoirs within five miles of Wemyss Bay. Then there was Loch Thom to the north east and the larger Gryfe Reservoirs further to the east of this.

DCI Bevan had already informed her that the DCS wouldn't release the funding to search these areas for Ross's body. There wasn't enough evidence to suggest he'd been murdered. Besides, the man could have been dumped in the sea just as easily as in these lochs.

But Alice had a feeling that the poor teacher was weighted down at the bottom of either Daff or Crawhin. These were the two bodies of water closest to Wemyss Bay. It fitted with their killer's MO that the disposal site would be near to where Ross had last been seen.

Despite her annoyance with Tony, she wasn't feeling aggrieved enough to inform his parents of their son's sexuality. Alice preferred to have the threat of that possibility in her back pocket for the next time they interviewed him. But she was keen to talk to the couple. The detective flicked over the pages of her file and sought out their contact details.

Chapter 40

The day was clouding over. Andy hadn't intended to come back to this house again so soon, but it couldn't be helped.

Mae was expecting him. She opened the door with a thin smile, standing back to allow Calder to enter. When he glanced at his uncle's widow, he wondered what had made him lust after her so passionately. The woman just seemed brittle and full of melancholy to him now.

'Did you manage to dig anything out?' Andy asked, without any preamble.

Mae led him into the living room, where a tea chest had been placed in the centre of the floor. 'This is it. Gavin brought it in from the garage last night. I sent all of Don's clothes to the charity shop. These items were the things I packed up when we moved out of the old house. I thought the kids might want to sort through it when they were a bit older.'

Andy experienced a surge of anger to see the way the chest had become saturated with damp and the cobwebs had gathered in the corners. It hadn't even been covered with a dust sheet.

Sensing his dark mood, Mae slipped silently out of the room into the kitchen, busying herself with preparing some coffee for them both.

Calder took out the items one by one. They were mostly books and vinyl records. The sight of them made him smile. As a rule, men weren't great collectors of sentimental items, like letters and cards. Don was no different. A few albums of Panini football stickers were all that remained of his childhood.

Then Andy reached the items relating to St Columba's Football Club. There were piles of dog-eared programmes, tied together with string. Don had obviously been reading the biographies of their greatest players, the copies of which were lying discarded amongst the rest of the stuff. Underneath this layer of books and football magazines were Don's files. Andy lifted these out carefully. He had no idea that his uncle had collated all of his notes from the articles he wrote for the Paisley Post so carefully.

Mae came into the room with a tray. She placed Andy's mug on the table. The woman edged slowly towards the articles laid out on the polished floor. Finally, Mae lowered herself to the ground, beginning to pick them up, flicking through the pages as if the contents might burn her.

'I didn't realise Don kept copies of all his articles for the paper. They're here in this binder.'

'Oh, aye. He was very proud of his writing. John and Liz were too young to read them at the time. I'll have to show them his pieces now. The editor loved Don, he really rated his work.'

Andy pulled out the last of the files and notebooks. 'Do you know where Don was writing his draft of the book about St Columba's? There's no sign of it here.'

Mae put her arms around her knees, like a wee girl in assembly. She crinkled her face in concentration. 'He wasn't writing the thing by hand. It was going on the computer. We had one with a big monitor back then. It took up the whole desk in John's room. Don used to tap away at it for hours in there, even when the boy was asleep.' She smiled.

'Then where is the draft copy? Have you still got that computer?'

Mae shook her head. 'Och, I've no idea what

happened to it. When we all got laptops it probably went on the tip. Sorry.'

Andy sighed. 'It's most likely not important anyway. I just know how much that book meant to Don. When you reminded me about the amount of time he was spending on it in the weeks before he went missing, I got an inkling it could be significant.'

'A copper's instinct,' Mae muttered. 'A feeling in your stomach.' She looked up and caught his eye. 'That was the feeling I had about Don not having killed himself. I couldn't prove it, but I just knew.'

'Then you had me and my Da' insisting he'd thrown himself into White Cart Water.'

'It made sense at the time.'

Calder shuffled closer to her. 'When the polis talk about a copper's gut feelings, they don't really mean it's anything supernatural. It's usually something concrete that the copper has picked up on. They've sniffed something out amongst the evidence. Did that happen with you, Mae? Was there a reason why you didn't believe that Don had taken his own life?'

Mae blinked several times. 'Well, I knew about Don's struggles with his sexuality and how terribly low he could become, but that wasn't what I'd been sensing from him in those weeks before the Glasgow Fair in 2005.'

'Then what was it that you'd noticed about Don?'

'It wasn't that he was depressed. It was more that he was jumpy, forever looking over his shoulder at imaginary shadows.' She reached out to touch Andy's arm. 'I think that he was afraid. Very, very afraid.'

Chapter 41

'Where have you been?' Carol asked abruptly, as Andy entered the kitchen of their flat, to find her seated at the table. The place was quiet. Amy was still at nursery school.

He frowned. 'I was at Mae's house, going through a box of Don's belongings. I told you this morning, remember?'

She nodded. 'Yes, of course. It's just that when I returned from the shops, I found this note stuffed under the door.'

Instinctively, Calder opened a drawer and took out a packet of disposable plastic gloves. He pulled them on before touching the crumpled paper. The note had been written in black felt tip. The spelling was awful, but he knew that was most likely deliberate.

'Do you know what your husband gets up to when he goes out at night? I do. It's disgusting and sick. Get yourself a real man and a proper dad for that pretty daughter of yours. He's bad news.' Calder felt the blood rush to his cheeks. 'What time did you find it?'

'I got back from the shop about eleven. It was there then. I hadn't seen anyone hanging around, so whoever posted it was gone.' She stared hard at him. 'What does it mean?'

Andy slipped onto the seat beside her. 'I don't know, love. It's just some nutcase. I deal with them every day at work. I suppose there's a chance a lowlife I arrested once has got hold of my address.'

'But this person knows about Amy.' Carol put a hand up to her mouth. 'That man who was hanging around the playground. He was watching me. Do you think this note is from him?'

Andy laid his hand on her arm. 'Why would it be?'

'I don't know.' Carol looked down at her lap. 'A few weeks back, you were working late nearly every night. There were times you didn't get home until the early hours of the morning. That time you said you were with DCI Bevan, I called her. She told me you'd been there all evening. I knew she was lying. Her first loyalty is to you, not us. Is that what this is about? Have you slept with another man's wife and now he's out to get revenge?'

Calder managed to take a deep breath and place his arms around her. 'I was going through a difficult patch, what with Don's disappearance getting raked up all over again. I spent a few nights just driving around Paisley in the car. Other times I walked along the river bank. I didn't know where I was going or what I was doing.'

She nodded, burying her face into his shoulder. 'Are you back with us now?'

Andy squeezed her tight. 'Of course I am. I love you, I love you both.'

*

Andy had secured the letter into an evidence bag. It was sitting on top of the ring binder of notes that Mae had allowed him to take away from her place. Calder's mind kept drifting back to the day they had Sunday lunch at the Mortimers' house. His nephew, John, had been watching him and Mae arguing in the kitchen. Andy couldn't help but worry that the note might have been sent by him.

To John, the notion of his cousin sleeping with his mum would certainly appear disgusting and sick. Calder thought it probably was. The idea of the lad being so eaten up by it that he'd send an anonymous note to Carol made him feel bad. He'd have to think of a way of setting things right with John. For now, Andy was so preoccupied with getting into Don's head during the summer of 2005 that it didn't seem a priority.

Calder's uncle had made a great deal of notes about St Columba's. He'd been focussing on the period during the early to mid-1990s, when the club's fortunes were growing and they'd moved away from their ground on the outskirts of Paisley to the newly built stadium just off the M8. Andy's own fondest memories were of going to the matches at the old ground, with its uncovered terraces and tiny bar. It had cost about ten times less for a season ticket too. If he were going to take Amy for a game, it would have to be a one off treat.

Calder got the sense that Don hadn't been keen on the move either. These handwritten documents catalogued escalating costs and delays by planners and building contractors. Andy thought it was no bloody wonder the ticket prices had to go up. St Columba's Park was completed towards the end of '96. It received another refurb in 2003, when a new hospitality wing was built. This addition had a corporate sponsor, Walmer Beers and Spirits, a company based locally. Don had scrawled *two million* next to the name of the firm, suggesting to Calder that this was the amount Walmer had donated to the build.

The remainder of the notes related to St Columba's fortunes on the pitch, the various transfers that took place and the proliferation of non-Scots players on the team. The research that

Don had carried out seemed to include the 2004/5 season. Calder concluded that his uncle must have been ready to complete the project. He wondered if Don would have saved his work onto a floppy disk. Then Andy considered whether USB sticks were in use a decade ago. He wasn't sure. These days, it would all be on some kind of cloud.

Carol came into the room and placed a bottle of beer on the table next to Andy. He glanced up and said thanks. Picking up the bottle he noticed it was a Walmer brand, with a picture of some fat monk by a barrel of hops on the label. Carol always bought the beers that were on offer in the supermarket. It wasn't usually Calder's kind of thing. The detective looked back at Don's notes. He felt that itch he got when the evidence was trying to tell him something. Andy took a swig of his drink. It was warm and strong tasting, but still hit the spot. 'What did you find out Don?' He muttered, as if the man was sitting next to him. 'And just what the hell happened to your book?'

Chapter 42

Michael Lomond was tending his neat front garden when DCs Clifton and Mann pulled up outside. The house was square and imposing. A sensible mid-range Volvo was parked on the driveway.

Alice saw a flicker of movement at one of the windows before Rosemary Lomond opened the front door and stepped onto the path to greet them. Her husband barely glanced up from his labours.

'Would you like to sit out in the garden? The weather is glorious.'

'Whatever suits you,' Alice replied affably. She didn't wish to ruffle the couple's feathers so early in the proceedings.

They were led down a side passage into a large garden with a rectangular lawn which stretched away into the distance. Dan took a seat at a wooden patio table shaded by an umbrella.

'I'll fetch us some refreshments.'

When the woman had disappeared through the patio doors Dan commented, 'nice place. I thought the shipyards all closed decades ago.'

'Most of them did,' Alice said. 'But Mr Lomond worked at one of the last. It pretty much had the monopoly on the government's naval orders. After retiring, he did some consultancy for a few oversees military contractors. I expect he raked it in then.'

Rosemary returned, with a teapot and a selection of china cups. 'I'll be Mum!' She set about fussily pouring the weak tea and offering them milk and sugar.

'Will your husband be joining us?' Alice asked

politely.

'Oh, when he's finished.'

'As I explained on the phone, we have reopened the case into the death of Mr Douglas Ross. He taught your son, I believe?' Alice sipped her drink politely and gazed innocently at their host.

'Yes, that's right. He was Tony's science teacher. He'd taught him since his first year in the senior school. The man was swept away whilst searching for rocks at Wemyss Bay, wasn't he? Gosh, it was *years* ago now.'

Alice looked at Rosemary Lomond closely. She wore a billowing floral dress and her hair was pure white, but the woman had a childlike aura about her. 'Did you know Mr Ross well?'

'Only from parents' meetings. He also took Tony's class on a fossil hunt once. That was Mr Ross's thing.'

'Did Tony like him?'

'I believe he did. Tony thought he was kind. Our son had difficulties fitting in at Wemyss College. He was a fragile little boy and the others were very sporty and enjoyed rough play. Mr Ross was one of the more sensitive teachers. Actually, I think Tony was really quite upset when he found out the man was dead. He suffered some sleepless nights.'

'Did you ever consider moving your son to a different type of school?' Dan addressed the woman directly.

Her face became puzzled, as if such an idea had never occurred to her before. 'The College was the making of him. Michael insisted he brave it out. As soon as Tony got into rowing in the sixth form he was a diffcrent person. Finally, he was on an equal footing with all those bigger, stronger lads.' Rosemary was positively glowing with pride.

They heard the gravel crunch along the side path.

Tony's father emerged from the shadows, looking flushed and sweaty. He sat at the table and helped himself to tea from the pot.

'It will be cold by now, darling. Why don't I make us some more?' Rosemary began fiddling with the cups and saucers.

'It doesn't matter,' he snapped. 'I only want to wet my palate.'

Alice could see the strong resemblance between this man and his son, except the detective suspected that Michael Lomond had always been solidly built. 'My name is DC Mann and this is DC Clifton,' she announced. 'We are here to ask you and your wife some questions about Mr Douglas Ross. He went missing eighteen years ago.'

Lomond cast a supercilious glare at the detective. 'What on earth can you imagine we might be able to tell you about *him?*'

Alice felt her hackles rising. She tried to mask it. 'We are trying to speak with everyone who had a connection to Mr Ross. Your son informed us that he held the man in high regard.'

A shadow passed across his ruddy features. 'Not that I recall. Tony was more of a sportsman than a scientist at that age. He trains the students at the university rowing club now, you know, and won a good few cups himself when he was an undergraduate at Aberdeen.' Michael puffed out his chest.

Alice was suddenly put in mind of Cock Robin in the nursery rhyme, before he was slain by the arrow. 'Well, we must have been mistaken. Sorry to have taken up your time.'

The detectives both stood.

'Thank you for the tea, Mrs Lomond. We'll see ourselves out,' Alice said.

Rosemary gawped at them. 'If you're sure that's

all?'

Alice nodded and they made for the passageway before she turned and added, 'Oh, by the way, did you know that your son was acquainted with Nathan McLaren, the man who was murdered on the Saturday of the Glasgow Fair weekend? We thought it was a funny coincidence, that he also had a connection with Mr Ross. Especially now the investigation into the teacher's disappearance all those years ago has been reopened.'

The delicate china cup that Michael Lomond was holding to his lips fell to the concrete patio and smashed into dozens of pieces. As the detectives walked back to the car they could hear the sound of Rosemary Lomond rushing around, frantically trying to clear it all up.

*

'Sorry,' Alice said, as they drove back to headquarters. 'I couldn't resist that. The man was just so bloody pompous.'

Dan puffed out his cheeks. 'Can you imagine coming out to that pair? Mrs Lomond probably doesn't even know that homosexuality exists and the husband most likely believes that all gays should be strung up. No wonder Tony hasn't told them.'

Alice kept her gaze fixed dead ahead. 'Do *your* parents know that you're gay?'

'Aye, I told them just after I left for university. It took a little while for them to adjust. We're all used to it now. Mum worried about me when I joined the police. She thought I'd get grief if anyone found out.'

'Is that why you never said?'

Dan glanced sideways. He was smiling. 'It's just no one else's business. Do I ever question you about your sex life?'

'No, but that's because I haven't got one. Have

you?' She enquired as an afterthought.

Dan chuckled. 'Not really. That's what makes this whole thing so silly. My sexuality isn't what defines me. I don't even want a boyfriend right now.'

'Well, that gives us both something in common.'

'What did you make of the Lomonds?'

'I think you're right and Tony's mum hardly knows what day of the week it is, but the dad could be hiding something.'

'I agree. He didn't want us making any kind of connection between his son and Douglas Ross.'

'Which just makes me want to keep digging even further.'

Chapter 43

A parade of students spilled out of the Halls of Residence. Calder caught sight of John, tall and lean, with a blond girl on his arm. Andy assumed this must be Shiona.

'John!' He called out, jogging over to intercept him. 'I was hoping to catch you.'

The young man cast him a guarded look. 'Hi Uncle Andy, is something the matter?'

'No, I wanted to talk, that's all.' He addressed the girl. 'I'm John's cousin and a friend of the family.'

'I'm Shiona, pleased to meet you.'

'Can I take you both for a coffee somewhere?'

John turned to his companion. 'Do you mind if I go alone with Andy? We've got some family stuff to sort out.'

'Of course not. I'll see you back in Halls later.' The young woman smiled at the detective and walked away. She struck Andy as the easy going type. He was glad. They were the best girlfriends to have.

'She seems very nice.'

'Aye, she is.' John led them towards the campus cafeteria, clearly wishing to get this meeting over with quickly.

Andy bought them a couple of Americanos, surprised at how expensive they were and marvelling at the number of students able to afford the prices. 'Did your mum tell you that I've been looking through your dad's belongings? I'm trying to piece together his movements in the weeks before he died.'

He nodded. 'Mum said.' He stared into the cup. 'Are you hoping to find out who killed him?'

'I'm not hoping, John. I will. But I need to know everything about what happened back then, in 2005, before I can do that.'

He looked up. 'Lizzie and I were only little. I can barely remember Dad now.'

'Your mum recalled that Don was writing his book on the computer in your room. Sometimes he'd stay on in there whilst you were asleep.' Andy spent a few moments emptying a packet of sugar into his drink, not wanting to appear to be putting pressure on the lad.

'Yeah, I used that computer to do my homework when I went up to High School. We had it for years. I *kind* of remember Dad using it too.'

'He was working on the book about St Columba's. Did Don ever discuss it with you?'

'We talked about the footie a lot. I was nine back then and mad on it. That's what Dad and I had in common, separate from Mum and Lizzie, I mean.'

To Andy's great dismay, he saw John's eyes begin to fill with tears. 'I'm sorry, son. I really didn't mean to upset you.'

'You coming barging into our lives again could hardly do otherwise. And what was all that with Mum the other day? Why was she backing away from you in the kitchen like that? It looked as if she was frightened of what you might do to her.'

'We were just arguing about your father, that's all. It's been a difficult time for all of us. But Mae and I have made things up now, everything's okay. We're going to work together to plan the funeral.'

John crossed his arms over his chest and adopted a stubborn expression. 'I don't see what the point is in having some poxy ceremony. All we've got to bury is a bag of old bones. It's hardly Dad, is it?' The young man's voice was starting to rise and other students were glancing over at their table.

'It's important to say goodbye to him. Your mother's waited a long time to be able to do it. She needs you to be there, supporting her.'

'Mum's got Gavin.'

'It's you and Lizzie she'll be really wanting by her side on that day.'

John looked him in the eye. 'Will *your* mum and dad be coming to the funeral?'

Andy shifted awkwardly in his seat. 'I honestly don't know. But Carol and Amy will be and my sister Kathy too.' He tried to assess John's reaction when he mentioned Carol. The lad's expression was difficult to read.

'Well, if Jack's not going and he was like a father to Dad, then I don't know why the hell I should.'

Andy wanted to reach across and take the boy by his collar, giving him a bloody good shake. 'You'll go because Donny was your da',' he hissed. 'Your own flesh and blood. Somebody took him away from us before he had a chance to watch you and Lizzie grow up. He adored the two of yous, worshipped the very ground you walked on. That's why you'll be going to his funeral laddie, even if I have to drag you there myself.'

*

When Mae called the flat later that evening, Andy thought he was going to get a row. Instead, John's mother thanked him. Her son had gone round to the house in Paisley after his shift at the student bar was over. They discussed the funeral arrangements. John said he'd spoken with Calder, who'd encouraged him to get more involved. Mae admitted that her son hadn't really hit it off with Gavin. The lad occasionally needed the advice of a man he truly respected and looked up to. Lizzie accepted Gavin as her father very quickly after he came into their lives but John never had.

Calder told her he was always willing to offer advice to John and a shoulder to cry on if necessary. They ended their conversation on good terms. As he returned to the sitting room and squashed up next to Carol on the sofa Andy felt quite sure that the note stuffed under the door had come from his young cousin, angry and frustrated after hearing the news that Don's body had been discovered and lacking a father figure to supply him with the guidance he so desperately required at this important stage in his life.

Calder resolved to say nothing to the lad about it. Tomorrow, he'd put the scrap of paper away in a drawer and forget it was ever sent, concentrating instead on the more urgent matter of tracking down Don's killer.

Chapter 44

DCI Bevan had been avoiding making contact with her dad. She knew he was busy helping to organise the summer show at Scalasaig and Huw Bevan understood that when his daughter had a murder case on he may not hear from her for weeks at a time. Dani had taken advantage of these circumstances to maintain radio silence.

DCs Mann, Clifton and Hendry had been working hard to demonstrate a connection between Tony Lomond and the three victims, but so far, the evidence chain was weak. Lomond was undoubtedly too young to have killed Ross and there was no suggestion that the young academic had ever come into contact with Donald Calder. They had a list of bars that Calder frequented as a young man, but Lomond would still have been at school during those years. Their paths couldn't really have crossed.

Dani sat at the table in the kitchen of her flat cradling a glass of single malt. It was still very light outside and she'd left the patio doors open. For some reason, the DCI couldn't shake the details of the west London murders of the late 1980s from her mind. Something about the original investigation had left her feeling troubled.

She downed the last of the whisky and reached for her mobile phone with a heavy sigh. The person she was calling answered quickly. 'I'm sorry to bother you in the evening, but I'd like to meet. Do you know the Winged Chariot on Gibson Street? Great, I'll see you there in half an hour.'

*

Professor Morgan was already seated at one of the private booths when Dani arrived. He wore a burgundy jumper and cords, a pint of dark ale gripped in both hands. The man looked apprehensive, wary perhaps. Bevan bought herself a glass of wine before joining him.

'I'm sorry,' he said, as soon as the detective slid onto the bench opposite. 'I was very rude the last time we met. I don't actually behave like that normally.'

'You told me exactly what you thought, Professor. It's a very rare experience in the modern world. I expect you shouldn't be apologising for it.'

Morgan shook his head. Dani noticed he'd had a haircut. She could now make out the strength of his jawline and his high set cheekbones. Those striking blue eyes were set off more appropriately. The man might even have been handsome when her mother knew him, all those years ago.

'I was blaming you for things that happened when you were just a young child. For a psychologist, that is simply unforgivable. I'm glad you called, because I'd like us to start again, if that's possible.'

Dani sipped the wine. 'I don't even know what you mean by that. I'm perfectly happy to work with you, Professor. You are still on the Home Office list.'

Morgan smiled ruefully, muttering, 'just like your mother.' More stridently he added, 'will you permit me to tell you a little about myself and how my life turned out after Moira had returned to you and your father?'

'Of course.' She was genuinely interested.

'I put in for a transfer almost immediately, spending the next decade teaching at the Russell Institute in London. That is where I met my wife,

Lavinia. We married in '88 at St Bride's Church on Fleet Street. Our sons were born in the early nineties.'

Dani peered at him curiously, he hadn't struck her as a man who had a woman at home to look after him and advise him on how he was presenting himself to the world.

'You're right, DCI Bevan. Lavinia and I aren't together any longer. She lives in Canada now with her second husband, but the boys are here in Britain. They aren't long out of university and stay with me often. So, you see, I'm not as pathetic and bitter as I've no doubt been making out. I had a good life after Moira turned me down. I was deeply in love with Lavinia for many years and wouldn't be without my sons for the whole world.'

'It was just that being thrown together with me, after all that time had passed. It was a shock.'

'Yes, something like that. But I'm very glad to have made your acquaintance, Danielle Bevan, and to see what an impressive life you've made for yourself.'

For one awful moment, Dani actually thought that Morgan was going to say how proud her mother would have been. Thankfully, he didn't and the DCI was spared the humiliation of bursting into floods of tears.

Instead, he tipped his head to one side and said, 'but this isn't why you wanted to meet this evening. There's something else you wanted to talk to me about?'

'I've been reading your book.'

'The one about Ian Cummings?' He shifted forward, resting his elbows on the dark wood.

'I was interested in the police investigation into the murders. Did you meet any of the investigating officers before you wrote it?'

'Yes, I spent a few weeks liaising with the Met. They were very cooperative with my research. I don't find that's always the case.'

'Did you ever speak with Harry Kyle, the DC who took part in the sting operation that resulted in Cummings' arrest?'

'No. Kyle was already living in New Zealand by that time. I had to use the case reports and the testimony of the other men who'd been at the flat in White City that evening.'

Dani reached inside her bag and pulled out a copy of Morgan's own book. She flicked ahead to the glossy pages of photographs in the middle. 'This is Ian Cummings at the time of the murders. He was tall, certainly, but not very well built. If you look at the later pictures, you can see that Cummings has obviously been building up his physique in prison.'

The professor nodded slowly, as he compared the two pictures. 'Yes, I can see that.'

'And here's a photo of Harry Kyle, taken in '89. The guy was pretty fit, and muscly too.'

'Okay, what's your point?'

Dani looked serious. 'It just doesn't ring true to me that Ian Cummings would have been able to attack Kyle in that flat and disable him so straightforwardly.'

'Well, he didn't, did he? Kyle was able to crawl into the bedroom and activate his police radio.'

'Yes, but he sustained some nasty wounds in the assault. I would expect a bulky, well-trained officer like Kyle to be able to take on the malnourished Cummings with relative ease.'

Morgan furrowed his brow. 'So what are you suggesting?'

Dani let out a breath. 'I don't think Cummings carried out those murders on his own. I believe he had an accomplice.'

Chapter 45

Rhodri Morgan carried the drinks back from the bar and set them down on the table, retrieving a couple of packets of nuts from his pocket to add to the haul.

'There was the key-cutter,' Morgan asserted. 'He was an accomplice of sorts and received a five year sentence for his involvement. He was out in two.'

'But he played no part in the murders themselves. I'm talking about another individual who was present in those flats when the men were tortured and killed.'

'The detectives at the time never considered that a possibility. If there *was* another man involved, why didn't Kyle say so? He was the only victim to survive.'

'That's what I can't work out. The man left the force pretty soon after it all happened and has never given an interview about the case, as far as I can gather. I'd really like a chance to speak with him.'

'Harry Kyle has been in New Zealand for twenty five years, I don't rate your chances.' Morgan sipped his pint thoughtfully. 'The only other person who would know is Cummings himself.'

'What's he like?'

Morgan set the glass down decisively. 'A liar and a sociopath. I wouldn't trust a single word that left his lips.'

'So what kind of man would Cummings protect? If there was an associate, then Cummings has been shielding him for all these years, taking the blame for the crimes himself.'

The Professor gave a thin smile. 'That's where

your theory falls down, I fear. Ian Cummings is utterly selfish. I can't see him putting another's needs ahead of his own. He simply isn't capable of it. In my clinical opinion, of course.'

'Could you do me a favour?'

'Yes, what is it?'

'Would you re-examine the notes you made of your interviews with Cummings. Can you see if he said anything at all that hints at the role of another individual in these crimes?'

'I'll take a look, if you want me to. But if you don't mind me saying so, shouldn't you be focussing all of your attention on the murders here in Glasgow?'

'My team are doing an excellent job on that, Professor Morgan. Somehow, my instincts are telling me to dig deeper into the London killings. I have a hunch it will help us with our current case.'

'Well, you're the detective.' He raised his glass. 'And I'm happy to follow orders.'

*

Bevan had already run a data check on Harry Kyle. He'd joined the Metropolitan Police in 1983, becoming a detective after five years on the beat. He left the force in late 1989, emigrating to Christchurch, New Zealand, with his new wife, Samantha.

Kyle would now be fifty years old. Dani wheeled her seat closer to the desk and logged onto the police personnel database. Fortunately, the system had been automated for a long time and DC Kyle's details were still recorded on the files. The addresses would all be out of date but it at least provided the DCI with the names of Kyle's next of kin in the UK.

It took only a matter of minutes to look up Kyle's

mother, Maureen. She'd attended a road safety seminar after committing a speeding offence three years ago. There was an address listed in east London. Bevan wasted no time in calling the number.

'Hello?'

'Good morning, is that Maureen Kyle?'

'I don't want to buy anything.' The woman's voice was weak and crackly.

'I'm not selling, Mrs Kyle. My name is Detective Chief Inspector Bevan from the Glasgow division of Police Scotland. I'm trying to track down the whereabouts of your son, Harry.'

'My son's not in the police anymore. He hasn't been for years.'

'I realise that. I simply need to speak with him about an old case he worked on. Harry isn't in any trouble. Do you have the contact details for him in New Zealand?'

There was a moment's silence. 'They're in Romford.'

'I beg your pardon?'

'Harry and Sam moved back here when my Alf was diagnosed with cancer. It was ten years back now. The kids were about to start at secondary school so it seemed like a good time.'

Dani's heart began to pump energetically. 'Could I have a phone number for them?'

'Well, I'd have to be sure of who you were first now wouldn't I?'

'Absolutely, Mrs Kyle. I will direct you to the Police Scotland website. Ring the number at the top of the page and ask the receptionist for me by name. They'll be sure to put you straight through.'

Chapter 46

Caitlin Hendry was becoming frustrated. She'd spent the entire morning looking into the background of Michael Lomond, like DC Mann had instructed her to. Tony's father was a retired executive who had led an extremely boring and completely blameless existence. Hendry couldn't understand why on earth they were spending so much time on this line of enquiry.

When Alice had left her desk to go for lunch, Caitlin moved across to take the chair opposite Dan Clifton. 'How are you progressing with the Douglas Ross case?'

Dan furrowed his brow. 'I'm going through all the witness statements from the original inquest. Then I'm planning to interview his son and daughter again. There must be some way of identifying his movements in the days leading up to his disappearance.'

'Do we really think anyone's going to remember what happened on a random March day eighteen years ago?'

'People recall more than you'd expect. Anyway, Caitlin, that's the job. A tiny little detail, one that seemed unimportant at the time, can break a case.'

The younger woman rested her face in her hands and stared at him. 'What if there was another way of going about this.'

'How do you mean?'

'The victims were all gay, right? So we're definitely looking for someone who targets homosexuals. The men who were singled out all lived in commuter towns on the outskirts of Glasgow with excellent train links to the centre of town. They *clearly* met their killer on the gay scene in the city somewhere. We've drawn a total blank with the fairgrounds and traders on Glasgow Green.' Caitlin paused, looking suddenly awkward.

'So, what's your thinking?'

'You're familiar with the gay scene, right? That's got to provide an advantage for us. Our perpetrator has got a thing about married men, what with this whole wedding ring ritual he's got going. So why don't we get you a gold band to wear and you can spend a few nights out in town, see if we can't flush this guy out of his dirty little burrow. We've even got that list you compiled, of the places Donald Calder frequented with his old boyfriend.'

Dan stopped what he was doing. 'The boss wouldn't like it.'

'Why not?'

'Because it's entrapment, or close enough. She's always said that's the last chance saloon for teams that have reached a total dead end. Even if the suspect gets caught out, which there's no guarantee of, it's incredibly difficult to build a case against them in court.'

'But imagine if we could get a *name* - a suspect other than Tony Lomond who we could actually put in the frame for *all* the murders. Then we would be able to throw ourselves into the spade work with a bit more enthusiasm.'

Dan pursed his lips. He did feel as if their investigation was treading water. This man could strike again at any time. Wasn't it better that *he* was the target, rather than an innocent member of the public?

Sensing he might be swayed, Caitlin added, 'I don't see what's wrong with you, me and Alice having a few evenings out on the town together. My dad never wears his wedding ring. To be honest, his finger's got too flabby to fit it on since he retired from the force. I can easily borrow it from the box and let you have it for the night.'

Dan was about to reply when DCI Bevan emerged from her office, gazing about the half empty floor. Noticing the two detectives at the nearby workstation she strode over. 'DC Clifton, DC Hendry, I'm catching a flight down to Stansted Airport this afternoon. DS Boag will be in charge whilst I'm gone.'

'Do you know how long you'll be away?' Dan asked.

'Not more than a couple of days. Keep Phil updated on any developments. I'm on the other end of my phone if you need me.'

When Bevan had disappeared behind the closing doors of the lift Caitlin pronounced, 'there you have it. Nothing to stop us from taking the initiative now.'

*

As Dani's taxi took her out of the parched, rolling corn fields of north Essex and into the built up hinterlands of the London commuter belt, she noted how much warmer it was down here than in Glasgow.

The sun was glowing within a hazy, cloudless sky and the air was thick with afternoon heat. It didn't take long before the cab was pulling up outside a semi-detached property on a leafy street in the town of Romford, a place which appeared to nestle within a criss-cross of busy roads and railways lines. Dani was immediately struck by how different this habitat must be to where the Kyles had lived in New Zealand.

Harry Kyle opened the door. He was still a big

man. His muscles bulged within a sleeveless shirt, his upper arms displaying a mesmerizing array of intricate tattoos. His hair was almost gone, making him look intimidating. 'Come inside,' he said flatly.

The house was nicely decorated. Harry led Bevan into a newly fitted kitchen.

'I'll make some coffee, Ma'am.'

Dani was surprised at his formality, but then she knew that old habits were hard to break for cops, no matter how long they'd been away from the force. 'I apologise for descending on you at such short notice.'

Kyle shook his head, a rather sad smile on his lips. 'Actually, I've been expecting you to come for about ten years. Or someone like you.'

Bevan tipped her head to one side inquisitively.

'Well, this *is* about the west London murders isn't it? Cummings *must* be due for release pretty soon.'

'The psychiatrists want him to stay in Broadmoor indefinitely. They believe he feels no remorse for his crimes.'

A dark shadow passed across the man's face. 'I think they're right about that. Cummings is a monster.' He handed the DCI a mug. 'Then why are you here?'

'I've been reviewing the case. There are certain similarities to a spate of recent murders in Glasgow. I've got a few questions about the day you caught Cummings. Would you be willing to answer them?'

Kyle's response surprised her.

'I get a small pension from the Met. It isn't much, but it makes a big difference to me and Sam. I work as a bouncer down at the Kings and Queens nightclub in town. Sam is a nurse. We don't make much money. I've just started the repayments on this kitchen. Can it be taken away from me?'

'No, of course not. I give you my word. If you

cooperate with me now, your pension is safe.'

Kyle slipped onto the chair opposite. 'Okay then, ask away.'

Dani leaned in closer. 'Did you ever sense another presence in that flat when you were attacked by Cummings? You are a strong man, Mr Kyle and Cummings was thin and malnourished back then. I don't believe he can have committed all those murders by himself.'

'The other DCs and I thought the same, but our SIO was convinced there was only one perp.'

'It was an incredible risk for you to take part in that sting operation to lure out the killer. I would never sanction such a thing for any of my officers.'

Kyle sighed deeply. 'I was a young man then, ambitious and gung-ho. I didn't think twice about it. I'd joined the force for a bit of excitement.'

'Tell me what happened when you got back to the flat in White City?'

'The guys in the surveillance car out front hadn't given me the nod, so I thought there was no one inside. We'd been at it for days by then with no action so we'd all become complacent, I suppose. I changed my clothes in the bedroom and decided I needed to call Sam. She was getting pretty pissed off with the whole thing. As I lifted the receiver, I noticed a movement out of the corner of my eye. I'd just managed to shift slightly before a huge weight barged me to the ground.'

'Was that Cummings?' Bevan interrupted, in obvious disbelief.

Kyle ignored the query. 'This big bloke was pinning me down, with my face pressed to the ground and there were heavy blows falling repeatedly on my head. That's when I knew there must be two of them, because the one restraining me was using both hands to keep me still.' He was avoiding

Bevan's eye. 'I was completely at their mercy. The blows finally stopped. That's when the man on top of me started to grab at my trousers, as if he was trying to pull them down. I shouted out then that I was a police officer and there were others outside. That made him stop. Then, he whispered something in my ear.'

'What did he say, Harry?' Dani could see how hard this was for him.

'He told me that he was a very important man. He knew my boss and that if I ever breathed a word to anyone that he'd been there in that flat with Cummings he'd make sure I was driven out of the Met with no pension.' Kyle's voice became a whisper. 'He said he knew how to make sure I never spoke about what happened.'

'Did the man rape you?'

Harry shook his head, his eyes wet with tears. 'No, I thought he was going to. I was terrified. But what he did instead was to spare me. I was totally in his power for those few moments and I sensed that it gave him an enormous buzz. I was waiting for the worst, but then he released me and backed away. He must have taken off before Cummings did because I felt the blows raining down once more. This time, I was able crawl away towards the bedroom. That's when I pulled the radio off the bed and switched it on. Cummings scarpered after that and the guys caught up with him on the fire escape.'

'Did you recognise the other man's voice?'

'Yes, but I didn't know from where. I was absolutely certain then, as I am now, that he had the authority to do exactly what he'd said.'

'Could he have been a policeman?'

'I considered that possibility, but decided not. If he'd been on the force, he'd have known about the sting operation and I'm sure he didn't. I always imagined he was some high-up official in the Home Office, a faceless pen-pusher who held all the cards.'

'Why did you never say anything?' Bevan's words were devoid of recrimination.

'Because I believed his threat and because at the time it felt like he'd bought my silence. He could have subjected me to what would have been a fate worse than death for a macho young lad like me back then, but he didn't. I knew I needed to accept that reprieve and start again with Sam. If I spoke out, he'd come back for me and next time, he'd finish the job.'

'But you're speaking out now?'

'When we came back from New Zealand things had changed here in Britain. The news was full of reports of important people being prosecuted for abusing kids in children's homes and that. I thought it was the right moment to tell the truth, that I might even be believed. I knew that Cummings would be due for parole. I swore that if anyone came asking, I'd tell them what really happened this time. In all these years DCI Bevan, you're the only one who ever has.'

Chapter 47

The atmosphere that day had been close and humid. The forecast predicted heavy rainstorms for the night. Carol had opened all the windows in the flat to their furthest extent. The skies hanging over the nearby housing estate were a dark, murky blue.

They'd shared a meal of salad and cold meats, but no one had much of an appetite. Carol was helping Amy to get ready for bed in the nursery as Andy stood by the kitchen window with a glass of cold beer in his hand.

Suddenly, he heard a distant door slam and a rush of tepid air gushed past his face. The wind was beginning to get up and it had become as dark as night. He pulled the latch closed, padding into the living room, planning to do the same to the windows in there.

The lights were off in this room. A flash of lightning outside abruptly illuminated the space. For a moment, Andy could have sworn he saw a figure seated on the sofa. When the flash came for a second time, he identified the dark shape as simply a haphazard pile of clothes Carol had brought out of the drier and left there before tea.

Andy smiled to himself, closing the windows and sliding open the vents, knowing that a downpour was imminent but that the temperature would remain very warm. As Calder made his way back to the kitchen, something caused him to pause and put his eye up to the spy hole in the front door. He leapt backwards, as if he'd been electrocuted.

There was a man standing directly outside their

flat. A black cap pulled forward to obscure his face. Andy glanced down the corridor, to make sure that Carol and Amy were still in her room. He peered out again, for longer this time. Calder slipped into the main bedroom for his baton. Then he slowly and deliberately opened up.

'John?'

The boy raised his gaze. 'Uncle Andy. I'm sorry to bother you. Can I come in?'

Calder stood back, allowing the lad to walk through to the lounge. 'Amy's just going to bed. We'll have to be quiet.'

'Yeah, sorry to come at this time. I know it isn't great.'

'Not at all. Like I told your mum, you're welcome here whenever you feel as if you need to talk. Do you want a beer?'

John shook his head. 'No thanks. I've been stood outside for ages. I didn't have the courage to knock.'

Andy indicated he should sit down. He slid the baton down beside the sofa and joined him. 'What's on your mind, son?'

Carol popped her head around the door, crinkling her forehead in puzzlement.

'Could you put the kettle on for us, love?'

'Of course,' she replied kindly, making herself scarce.

John sat absolutely still. He seemed to be cradling something in his hands.

Calder's investigative antennae started to kick into life. 'What have you got there? Is it for me?'

The boy nodded. 'I wanted to give it to you straight away, when you started asking about it, but I've had it for so long I've become very attached to it. It's been my little piece of Dad – nothing to do with mum or Lizzie. He wanted me to have it. Dad said that if anything ever happened to him, he wanted me to have his book. For years I thought it might have been a dream, him whispering those words into my ear as I dropped off to sleep. But I knew in my heart it was actually real.'

'I think Don would want me to have it now.'

John glanced sideways at Calder. 'Aye, I think you're right.' He unfurled his fist. In the centre of the boy's sweaty palm lay a small, rectangular memory stick.

*

Dan, Alice and Caitlin rushed into the pub, their coats pulled over their heads to shield them from the torrential rain which was bouncing off the pavements of Sauchiehall Street.

'So, which one of yous lovely lassies am I supposed to be married to?' Dan asked with a grin, heading purposefully towards the shiny chrome bar.

'Neither of us, you numpty,' Caitlin shouted over the music. 'You'd hardly bring your wife along when you were cruising for men.'

'Oh aye, I see your point.' Dan got the drinks and brought them to a small table in the corner. He spotted a couple of people he knew and gave them an acknowledging nod, hoping they wouldn't come over for a chat. He didn't want to have to explain the wedding ring on his finger.

Alice had kept her jacket on, downing half her vodka and coke in one gulp. 'I really can't see the purpose of this. What are the chances of our man happening to be in the same places as us tonight?'

'That's why we're moving from one bar to another,' Caitlin explained impatiently. 'At least we're doing something pro-active.'

The detectives had already shared the details of their domestic arrangements and barely existent love lives. They were rapidly running out of things to say to one another. Alice sat back in her chair and observed the room instead.

'Watch out,' Dan said to his colleague. 'You're starting to look just like a cop.'

'I *am* a bloody cop,' she muttered. Then she leant forward again, squinting her eyes at the crowd. 'Is that Tony Lomond over there?'

Hendry and Clifton scanned the men's faces as surreptitiously as they could manage.

'No,' said Dan. 'I can see the bloke you mean. He looks a bit like him but he's a lot older.'

'Yeah,' Alice replied. 'I see what you mean. False alarm.' The DC sighed, picking up her glass and finishing off the drink in one final swig.

Chapter 48

It wasn't easy for Andy to find a machine where he could use the memory stick. Eventually, he and Carol found an old laptop in a cupboard, that they'd hardly used since both getting their tablets.

Calder powered it up, cursing the amount of time it took to chug into life. He had no idea if the ancient storage system on the little stick was still going to work. John admitted he hadn't loaded the contents for at least five years, not since they'd dumped their old computer.

The process was painfully slow, but eventually, a Word document appeared on the screen. Calder experienced a wave of emotion. Here were Donny's words - stuff that no one had read except his uncle himself and John. From what the boy had told him the previous night, he'd not really taken in much of what his father had written.

Andy glanced at the word count in the bottom left hand corner. 'Jeez,' he muttered solemnly. This was going to be a long haul.

*

DCI Bevan felt as if she'd wasted an entire morning at New Scotland Yard in London. The officers she'd been introduced to had been extremely helpful but absolutely no one she'd spoken to possessed any direct knowledge of the Ian Cummings case.

Finally, she was called into the office of Detective Superintendent Goldman, a man of sufficient rank to take her news seriously. Samuel Goldman remained seated as Dani entered his domain, simply reaching across with his hand as she took the chair opposite.

'I appreciate you giving me your time, Sir,' Bevan began.

The man had strikingly dark hair and hooded eyes that appeared almost black in colour. 'It sounds as if you may have uncovered a serious development. I've sent a couple of officers to take a fresh statement from Harry Kyle.'

'Are you familiar with the case?' Dani tried to assess the man's age but found it tricky to place.

'Yes. I was a detective constable back then and although I wasn't on the investigation myself, everyone at the Met knew what was going on. It was a media circus.'

'What do you think our chances are of finding this accomplice?'

Goldman pursed his lips. 'We'll do our best, of course, but from what you've said, Kyle's account doesn't provide us with very much. It all comes down to whether Cummings will give the man up. It seems incomprehensible that he hasn't done so up to now.'

'You should liaise with a psychologist based at Glasgow University called Professor Rhodri Morgan. He's interviewed Cummings extensively. My theory is that Cummings feels under the protection of this other man in some way. Perhaps he promised Ian special conditions and privileges in prison if he kept his existence a secret.'

'Do you believe this person really wields that kind of power and influence?' Goldman looked suddenly worried.

'Not necessarily, but he's used to manipulating people, young boys specifically. I suspect you need to begin your search for him in the children's homes that Cummings attended as a lad. I expect this individual groomed Ian from a young age. Perhaps he was a manager or an inspector in one of these institutions. Ian must have come to rely upon this person for protection. Or he's simply terrified of him. But somehow, I believe the relationship will be more complicated than that.'

A shadow passed across Goldman's jowly features. 'Of course, we must hope this man has not harmed others in the intervening years.'

Dani nodded, her expression grim. 'For what it's worth, I have a hunch that this second man's motives were sexual. He committed the indecent assaults on the victims. I think it was Cummings who did the killing. Ian wanted revenge on the types of men he felt had abused and taken advantage of him as a child. His accomplice was one of these men himself but he was also Ian's protector. They had a very complex dynamic.'

'Finding this man won't be easy.' Goldman sighed.

'No, but we have a duty to those poor victims to do our best to try.'

Chapter 49

Donald Calder had devoted several chapters of his book to the moving of St Columba's to its current site off the M8. Andy felt his eyelids drooping as he scanned through the pages. He wondered if Don had lost sight of what was important in this project and got bogged down in the detail. He couldn't imagine this section of the book being of any great interest to fans of the club.

Then, certain entries began to intrigue the detective. In the mid-nineties, the club had worked closely with west Renfrew council to obtain planning permission to take over a strip of industrial land that lay a quarter of a mile east of the motorway. The process was long and drawn out, but eventually, they'd been granted the necessary permission.

Despite the club's press releases, that claimed they had regenerated an ugly piece of wasteland to build St Columba's Park, creating dozens of new jobs for the area, Don had discovered that it wasn't quite so straightforward.

In 1995, the industrial site was occupied by an extensive traveller community, their caravans and equipment covering a significant area. Many of the children of the travellers attended local schools. Don had found evidence of protests being lodged by the community against the development, but their presence on the land was illegal and unpopular with nearby residents. They also lacked the resources to fight the football club's plans.

Calder could tell that his uncle's investigative journalist's instincts had kicked in at this stage in his research. The club and the council had, by 1996, reached a compromise with the travellers. Most of them were willing to take money to be rehoused in other parts of Scotland and those that chose to remain were given a plot, just a tiny proportion of their previous settlement size, in an area shielded off from the new development.

This had appeared to put an end to the dispute. Until the club found that they wanted to extend the ground once again, after the board were offered a hefty investment from Walmer Beers and Spirits in 2003. Two million smackers, to be precise. Then, the presence of that little encampment of travellers became much more of a nuisance.

Andy closed down the screen and logged off. He placed the memory stick in his trouser pocket, entering the hallway and grabbing a jacket. 'I'm just popping out for a while,' he called through to Carol in the kitchen, before stepping out of the door and closing it firmly behind him.

*

This time, when he pulled up at St Columba's Park, Andy didn't have an appointment. It was a Saturday afternoon and there were people milling in and out of the main gate. Calder walked in behind a family sporting purple and white scarves, ducking through a side door and striding down a corridor he recognised from the last time he'd been there.

When he reached Terry Finch's office, the detective didn't bother to knock. Finch half stood as Andy barged inside, a bottle of scotch placed unscrewed on the desk in front of him. 'Calder? What the hell...?'

'Guilty conscience, eh?' Andy tipped his head towards the bottle.

Finch narrowed his eyes. 'What are you doing here - is this an official visit, or should I be calling your superiors? I've got a lot of friends at your headquarters.'

'Oh, I'm sure you have, pal.' He stretched out his arms in a conciliatory manner. 'I'm here for a wee chat, that's all.'

Finch seemed to relax just a fraction. 'Then please take a seat. There's no need for animosity between us.'

Andy did his best to remain cool. 'I've been doing a lot of reading these past few days.'

A vein at the side of Terry's temple twitched. 'Oh aye, I didn't have you down as the studious type.'

Andy laughed. 'You've got that right, Terry. But Donny certainly was. In fact, I think a lot of folk underestimated him. Is that what it was like for you? I expect you thought Don was your typical local hack numpty, just the kind of nonentity to create a nice little whitewash history of St Columba's Football Club.'

'I've been extremely cooperative, Andy. But I think it's probably time you left now. Out of respect for your family, I wouldn't want there to be any trouble.'

Calder snorted. 'I don't believe you hold my family in particularly high regard.' He edged forward, gratified to see Terry withdraw from him ever so slightly. 'When Don came to see you, in the week before he died, was that the point at which he told you what he'd found out?'

Finch didn't bother to reply.

'In the summer of 2003, your board were becoming increasingly frustrated. You'd been pledged two million quid if you could build an entertainments terrace onto the park. But you knew full-well that as part of your 1996 planning agreement, a small traveller community were permitted to remain in the area you wanted to expand into. Donny smelt a rat whilst completing his research for the book in 2005 and decided to poke into your dealings a little more deeply.

He discovered that a fire had broken out at the traveller camp a couple of months before work began on your shiny new extension. An old couple were burnt to death in their caravan. It persuaded the council that the camp was unsafe and needed to be dispersed. This meant that your application was a shoo-in. A police investigation was launched. It concluded that the fire was caused by faulty electrics on the site. These kinds of tragedies happened all the time, they said.'

The blood had drained from Terry Finch's features. 'It's perfectly true. The investigators found it was just an accident.'

'But Don didn't like the feel of it, so he tracked down some of the old residents of the traveller site. He spoke to a few folk who were willing to testify to being harassed by men from the club who tried to intimidate them into leaving their homes. My uncle was piecing together a nice little exposé when he conveniently went missing, his body finally being discovered by my division, weighted down at the bottom of the reservoir.' Andy suddenly lunged forward, grabbing Finch by his collar and pinning him to the back wall of his own office. 'Did you have Donny killed, eh? If you don't tell me the truth right now, I swear I grind your skull into this corrupted, godforsaken brickwork.'

Chapter 50

Calder wiped his hands down his trousers as he stormed back to the car, feeling as if they'd been contaminated. He pulled away slowly, taking a long hard look at the buildings around him as he did so. Andy was certain that at least two people had died in order for the complex to be built. His da' was quite right when he said that moving out here had ruined the club he'd loved since boyhood.

But according to that scumbag Finch, Don's disappearance had nothing to do with him or his heavies. He'd been shitting himself that Don was about to bring the police into the investigation. Finch had tried to offer his uncle a payoff to silence him. But Finch swore on his kids' lives that it was as much of a surprise to him as anyone when Don disappeared that Saturday in July.

Finch said he was guilty of nothing more than being bloody relieved that Don was gone. Which to Andy was bad enough. So he poured the best part of a bottle of single malt over the guy's head. The bastard had it coming. The question of what Don had got himself involved in during those last days of his life still remained. At least the book had given Andy a good idea of what was going on in his uncle's head at that time. It was a start.

On his way home, Andy decided to stop for a drink. He parked up and walked the length of Sauchiehall Street. The Saturday revelries were already in full swing. He entered one of the quieter bars and sat at a table with his bottle of beer. For the first time, he considered sharing what he'd discovered with DCI

Bevan. It felt as if he had a solid new lead. Andy ran through the evidence in his head. Don had been digging into a possible deliberate arson at the St Columba Park that killed two travellers. In the process, he'd questioned several members of the traveller community that he'd tracked down. Was this how Don's path had crossed with his killer? Maybe he was planning to meet one of his contacts on the afternoon of the Glasgow Fair?

Calder had been lost in his thoughts and hadn't noticed a man approach him. He looked up. The guy was tall and handsome, perhaps a little older than Andy himself.

'Do you mind if I join you?'

'If you like,' the detective replied, thinking it might be a good idea to ask the regulars a few questions.

'Thanks,' the man responded affably. 'I couldn't allow you to sit there all on your own, especially looking so sad.'

*

It was a milder evening and the rain had cleared. Dan and Caitlin stood outside with the other drinkers, as they had at most of the pubs they visited. Alice had ducked out of this trip. She was spending the weekend at her parents' house in Largs.

'So you weren't tempted to go off to college, then?' Dan asked his colleague. 'You seem pretty dedicated to the force.'

Caitlin smiled. 'I didn't get on too well at school. I couldn't knuckle down to the academic stuff. I was more of an ideas and action kind of person. Besides, my dad was a detective. I was brought up on the whole police thing, riding around in my plastic cop car in the garden.'

'I can picture that.' Dan chuckled. 'Do you fancy another drink?'

The DC shook her head. 'I've had enough, thanks. This idea looks like it was a non-starter. There are dozens of clubs and bars in central Glasgow. Sorry I wasted your time.'

Dan laid a hand on the girl's arm. 'We've got to know each other better after a few nights on the town. No harm done, eh?'

Caitlin nodded. They picked up their jackets and made their way down the road, in the direction of the nearest subway station. For some reason, Dan's vision was drawn down one of the dimly lit side streets, where two men were shuffling along awkwardly; one having to support the weight of the other, almost dragging him in the direction of a parked car at the far end of the passage.

Dan stopped and nudged Caitlin's arm. 'That doesn't look right.'

The detectives entered the dark alley. Dan shouted to the men, asking if they needed any assistance. The more upright of the two turned his head, immediately picking up his pace. He hoisted the other guy higher onto his shoulder and manoeuvred his prone form more quickly towards the stationary vehicle.

Clifton broke into a run, but the man had already bundled his victim into the back of the car and was making for the driver's seat. As the door slammed shut, Dan reached the vehicle at full pelt, only managing to stop by pressing himself against the rear window, getting a good view of the unconscious person slumped inside.

The detective hammered his fists hard on the glass. 'Andy?! For Christ's sake, wake up!'

He didn't move a muscle.

The car's engine sparked into life. When the headlights flicked on, Dan's mouth dropped open in horror. Caitlin Hendry was standing with her legs apart, hands resting on the bonnet, as if to prevent the assailant's escape single-handed.

'Get out of the way, Caitlin!' Dan screamed.

She turned her head, managing to shift to the side ever-so slightly, just before the vehicle angrily spun its wheels and accelerated away fast, knocking DC Hendry to the cold, hard pavement like a solitary pin in a bowling alley.

Chapter 51

DCI Bevan didn't think she'd ever been so angry. It had taken half an hour for her to get from the ICU at the Glasgow Royal Infirmary to the Pitt Street Headquarters. This had at least given her some time to calm down.

Bevan strode single-mindedly across the floor of the serious crime division. 'Clifton and Boag, in my office. Now!'

Dan was the first to speak. 'How is she, Ma'am?'

'In a critical condition, DC Clifton. Caitlin has suffered a serious head trauma and has two broken legs. Her parents are currently performing a vigil by the young woman's bedside.' Dani looked from one man to the other. 'What the *hell* was she doing there?'

'It's no excuse, because you left me in charge,' Phil began, 'but I had no idea they were visiting the bars at night, Ma'am.'

Dani stared at Clifton. 'Who's idea was it?'

The DC visibly squirmed. 'It was something that Caitlin and I came up with between us.'

The DCI narrowed her eyes. 'Have we not worked together long enough for you to know that I would never sanction such a reckless operation? Phil tells me that you were sporting a *wedding ring* when they arrived at the scene. Been watching too much TV drama have we DC Clifton? You might well be watching at bit more from now on, and it will be of the daytime variety. But for now, I want to know everything about that vehicle and the man who abducted DC Calder.' She slammed her fist down hard on the table, unable to mask the waver in her voice. 'We need to track down that bastard, as soon as bloody possible.'

*

Bevan sat at the kitchen table with her hands clasped together, a mug of tea positioned untouched before her. 'Where is Amy?' She asked gently.

'At my mum's place.' Carol was very quiet and still, as if the news hadn't properly sunk in. 'Who would want to abduct Andy? It doesn't make any damn sense.'

'What had Andy been up to since he'd been on leave?'

'He was trying to find out everything he could about his uncle Don. Andy wanted to piece together his movements in the days before he died.'

'So he was still investigating the case. That must explain what he was doing in a gay bar on Sauchiehall Street.'

'Have any witnesses come forward?' Carol looked suddenly hopeful.

'A few folk saw them together in the Prince Edward. We have a decent description of the man who took Andy. He was tall, good-looking, but older than their usual clientele – mid-forties, perhaps. Have you seen anyone like that recently?'

Carol shook her head, tears escaping onto her cheeks. 'You know he went weird for a while. That time when I called your place to track him down. I know he wasn't really with you. Do you think he's upset somebody – is this the work of an angry *husband* who's out to get revenge?'

Dani reached across and took her hand. 'We're looking into every possibility. But I really don't think so. It seems that this man must have spiked Andy's drink, with Rohypnol perhaps. This doesn't strike me as the MO of a jealous husband. Have you got any solid reason to think Andy was having an affair?' Bevan felt guilty asking the question.

'There was a note, pushed under the door last week.' Carol recounted what it had said.

The DCI's mind was ticking over fast. 'Do you still have it?'

'I think Andy put it in one of the drawers in our room. I'll go and check.' Carol came back in a few minutes later, with the scrap of paper sealed up in its plastic covering.

'I'll need to take it,' Dani said carefully.

'Of course. And then there's the book.'

'What book?'

Carol explained their discovery of the draft version of Don's book. 'I know that Andy didn't save a copy, he didn't think it would be safe. I'm fairly sure he would've had the memory stick on him when he was taken.' The woman suddenly crumpled, as the reality of the situation finally hit home. 'Who's got him, Dani?' She sobbed, 'what the hell are they doing to him?'

Bevan moved over and placed her arms around her friend. 'I don't know Carol, I just don't know.'

Chapter 52

Bevan addressed her team. 'DC Calder was still investigating the murder of his uncle. He'd been visiting the places that Donald Calder had gone to in the days before his death. He'd recently discovered a draft copy of Donald's book on the St Columba Football Club. According to Carol, Don had uncovered some kind of corruption or dodgy dealing at the place through his research. He'd even confronted one of the directors about it.'

'Andy had discovered this not long before he himself was kidnapped,' Phil put in.

Dan stood up, clearing his throat. 'I knew that Andy was investigating his uncle's death. I bumped into him at the Lime Tree bar a couple of weeks back. We reached a kind of unspoken understanding. I wouldn't mention what he was up to and he wouldn't say anything about me being gay.'

Bevan took a deep breath, thinking she'd have to add it to the list of things she'd be holding DC Clifton to account for when this was all over. For now, they had other issues to concentrate on. 'What about the car – any news on that?'

Alice responded to this, 'the vehicle used last night was a Vauxhall Astra. From Dan's recording of the number plate we were able to ascertain it was stolen a few days ago from outside a house in Priesthill.'

'That's not far from Barrhead.' Dani frowned. 'Could this man be our serial killer?'

'I think that's very likely, Ma'am. Caitlin Hendry had the idea to flush out the murderer of Nathan

McLaren by using Dan as bait. It looks as if DC Calder had already done the same thing with his investigations, except this time, it was entirely unintentional.'

'Does that mean the unearthing of corruption at St Columba's Park has nothing to do with Andy's kidnapping? Is it a coincidence?'

'I don't think so.' Alice puffed herself up, looking confident. 'Something about it rings a bell from when Caitlin was researching the Glasgow Fair. I'd like permission to go back through her notes and check it out.'

'Of course. Get onto it straight away. In the meantime, we focus our efforts on examining the motorway CCTV footage on all routes out of the city centre last night after 11pm. I want to know exactly where that car was headed. If Andy is being held by the person who killed Douglas Ross, Donald Calder and Nathan McLaren, then we really don't have much time.'

*

The surroundings were cold and damp. Calder imagined that he was in some kind of cellar. It was definitely beneath ground level. His hands were bound behind his back and his ankles secured together with wire. A thick piece of tape was stuck over his mouth but it was already coming loose. Calder felt sick and his head was pounding, as if he had the almightiest of hang-overs.

The guy from the bar must have spiked his drink. For an experienced police officer, he'd been incredibly dim. But the tiniest glimmer of hope was alive in his mind. Andy could have sworn he made out a commotion in the distance as he got bundled into the car. Although he could barely move a limb, he'd seen Dan Clifton's face just before he slipped away into oblivion. If it hadn't been a hallucination, then it meant they knew he'd been taken. As long as Clifton was still alive, that was, and whoever had kidnapped him hadn't made sure the policeman couldn't follow. Andy tried not to allow that thought to invade his head. He could already feel hot tears forming in his eyes.

Calder focussed instead on recalling his conversation with the man who abducted him. The guy was talking about machinery. He was an engineer of some kind, he was proud of the skills passed down to him by his family. The chap was slick and believable, not your average serial-killer. A memory shot to the forefront of Andy's brain. He'd found him familiar. Whilst they were chatting, he'd decided the guy reminded him of someone. If only the pain in his head would subside for just a moment, then he might have a sporting chance of remembering who it was.

Chapter 53

Notes and printouts were spread in front of Alice at her work station. She'd not permitted any interruptions all morning. When DCI Bevan had mentioned St Columba's Park, the DC had recalled a detail from Caitlin's research.

When the St Columba's Park extension was built in 2003, another traveller community had been evicted from their site beside the M8 in order to make way for it. The council had been fully behind the decision. This information had turned up in the notes DC Hendry was sent by the Showmen's Guild.

Alice looked into it further. Caitlin had highlighted how the O'Driscoll family were dispersed from their site in 2007 due to a fire on the camp. This had ended their travelling fair business and resulted in part of the clan leaving for Europe on a permanent basis. She was amazed to discover, from the newspaper reports of the time, that something similar had occurred at the St Columba's Park site. In this case, a traveller couple died when several caravans were burnt to the ground. This prompted the council to declare the site unsafe and move the occupants on.

Was this the scandal that Don Calder was investigating before he was killed? Alice wondered. In both instances the police had ruled out foul play, yet there were businesses set to make a shed-load of money out of the traveller communities being moved on. In the case of the O'Driscolls, a housing developer had swooped in and built an executive estate on the site they'd been turfed out of.

Alice closed her eyes tight shut. Despite Don

Calder uncovering corruption and possibly even murder, it didn't seem as if he'd been killed by a person setting out to silence him. The connection here, which Caitlin had spotted early on, was with the travellers who ran the fairgrounds. Alice flicked her eyes open. Don must have interviewed people for his book. He must have spoken with traveller folk who'd been evicted by the council. It's what any decent investigative journalist would do. That's what brought Don together with his killer.

Douglas Ross and Nathan McLaren must have come into contact with this man, too. The fairground at the Glasgow Green could have been McLaren's contact point, but Ross was different. So what was it that connected *all* three men?

The DC jumped up, grabbing her jacket and heading for the lifts. 'I'm just popping out for an hour,' she called over to Dan, not waiting for his reply.

*

Tony Lomond was delivering a lecture. Alice waited outside until all the participants had left the theatre. They appeared to be predominantly overseas students. Teaching had become an all-year round profession these days. She approached Lomond at the front desk, where he was carefully gathering together his notes.

'Back for one of our pleasant little chats, DC Mann?' He barely looked up.

'Another person has gone missing. He's a good friend of mine.'

'Well, as you can see, I am going about my normal business, not kidnapping and murdering people.'

Alice felt her anger bubbling up. She reached

forward with her arm, brushing his notes, files and books onto the floor. Lomond turn to stare at her in amazement. 'What the hell are you doing?'

'A clever, brave young woman was knocked down last night, trying to save my friend from being abducted. She's in hospital in a critical condition.'

For the first time, Alice thought she saw a flicker of concern in Tony's eyes. 'What can I do? I'm not responsible.'

'We went to see your parents in Inverkip. They've got a lovely place there. Your mum was very hospitable. But for some reason, I don't think your dad was very pleased to see us.'

'Did you tell them about my connection to Nathan McLaren?' His face was ashen.

'Yes, but we didn't go into any great detail. Don't worry, your secret's still perfectly safe. For now, that is. But with this new development, a man being missing and in danger, I'm afraid that all bets are off. We'll probably have to question your father again. This time, we won't be treading on eggshells.'

Tony ran a hand through his hair. 'What do you want to know?'

'There's a connection between you and both Douglas Ross and Nathan McLaren. I don't believe you murdered them, but there's something here you're not telling me. I believe it's to do with your dad. He didn't like me asking questions. Why is that?'

The man sighed heavily and led Alice over to the rows of seating that stretched up towards the roof of the lecture theatre. They sat side by side.

'My life started out rather differently,' he began, staring down into his lap. 'Until I was four years old, I lived with my mother. She was called Orla O'Driscoll. She told people's fortunes at the travelling fairground that had been run by her family for decades. We had a caravan at a showmen's camp near Rutherglen. The families had lived on the site for generations. I stayed with Orla and my older brother, Liam. I still remember it well.'

'So how come you ended up with the Lomonds?'

'Michael is my father. He met Orla when she worked the fairgrounds out along the Clyde coast. The O'Driscoll's would set up in various seaside towns out there for the entire season. One summer in '83, my dad saw Orla at her stall near the seafront at Wemyss Bay. She was a very beautiful woman. Dad started an affair with her. I'm certain he gave her money, even back then, so I'm not sure how the relationship would be defined.'

'And Rosemary didn't know about it?'

Tony shook his head. Not in '83. 'After I was born, Orla informed my father he needed to support me financially, which he did for those first four years. Then something changed. Michael and Rosemary had been trying for a baby of their own for decades. I believe there'd been several miscarriages. The doctors told her they shouldn't try any more. Another pregnancy would kill Rosemary and the baby.'

'So your dad turned his attention to you.' Alice almost felt sorry for him.

'I think he told Rosemary about my existence then, and dad brought her to the travellers' camp to see me. Apparently, I looked just like Michael and it melted her heart – that's the story, anyway. Dad told Orla that he would give me a wonderful life; I'd go to a private school and have every opportunity I could possibly dream of. What mother would turn an offer like that down?'

'And your brother, he remained with Orla?'

'Liam? Oh aye, he was only my half-brother anyway. His father was long off the scene. Liam was a good decade older than me. He worked the rides at the fairground and helped support my mother. There was something about his real father that they never discussed. Orla had actually been married to him and Liam kept his surname, although my mother refused to use it and reverted back to O'Driscoll quick enough.'

'What was the name?'

'Hadley, Liam Hadley he's called.'

'Are you still in contact with Orla and Liam?'

Tony sucked in air through his teeth. 'I'm not supposed to be. It was part of the arrangement that Dad would pay them a lump sum and they'd never see me again. But of course Dad couldn't really enforce that. My birth mother knew where we lived. She always had the threat of tipping off Dad's bosses about my real parentage hanging over him. Dad and Rosemary don't have many family or friends. That's why it was easy for me to fit into their lives. I started at Wemyss College Preparatory School as soon as I went to live with them.'

'So you *did* still see Orla?'

'She turned up at the house every so often, sometimes with Liam and occasionally without him. Liam still contacts me from time to time. He *is* my brother after all.'

'Did Orla or Liam ever meet Mr Ross?' Alice tried to keep the urgency out of her voice.

Tony appeared surprised by the question. 'Why would they have?' Then he paused for a moment, as an unbidden memory played itself out silently across his features. 'Wait a second. There *was* a day when Liam came to see me at Wemyss Bay. It was fortunate, because Mr Ross had taken us for a fossil hunt down on the beach, otherwise I might not have seen him. Liam walked straight up to our group and started chatting to me. Mr Ross came over and asked who he was. He didn't want some stranger talking to one of his pupils, I suppose. I explained he was my brother and it was okay. But Ross lingered for a while, he seemed mesmerized by Liam. When he finally went away, I joked with my brother that Ross probably fancied him, because that was the talk of the boys' dorms back then. My brother was really good looking, you see, although he's not gay, like me. We've never discussed it, but I can just tell.'

Alice had stopped listening by this stage. 'I need the most recent address you have for Liam Hadley, and Orla O'Driscoll.'

Tony was lost now in the recollections of his sad life that Alice's questions had prompted. 'They all had to move away, after the motorway extension was built. Some tried to stay on in their caravans, where they'd lived all their lives and given birth to their babies. But there was a terrible fire, destroying everything they owned. That was an end to their way of life. Liam always claimed it was deliberate - the bastard developers trying to force them out. Well if it was, it worked. The community got broken up, completely dispersed. Liam and my mum ended up on a council estate near Priesthill. If you hold on here a second, I'll find you the address.'

Chapter 54

The pain surging through his lower back was getting worse. Calder didn't know if it was best to remain as still as possible or to try and shift about a bit. Despite the number of hours he'd been down in this place he didn't need the toilet, probably because he was dehydrated.

Then came the moment he'd been half praying for and half dreading. The door at the top of the steps creaked open. A narrow shaft of light swept out across the area below, revealing the full extent of the basement for the first time. There were barrels lined up in one corner and those green plastic crates you got in pubs, full of tiny bottles of fruit juice. Calder even thought he'd caught a glimpse of something beyond the door, a long corridor with a garishly patterned carpet. Within a few seconds, the source of light was extinguished.

Andy imagined that however it was had gone away again, but then he felt a blast of sour breath tickle his cheek.

'Are you comfortable?'

The voice was a woman's. Calder wasn't expecting that. He shook his head. No point in lying.

'But you can stay like that for a wee while longer?'

Andy nodded. He'd rather be uncomfortable than dead, that was for sure.

'Good, because I'm still busy upstairs. We've had a late rush on. Do you need the toilet?'

He shook his head again, vigorously.

'Right then, you'll keep.'

Calder unconsciously shuffled further into the

shadows, as the woman moved away from him and disappeared back into the darkness.

*

The street was very quiet for such a warm day. A few kiddies were out on their bikes in the middle of the road, riding round in circles, with one hand on the handlebar and the other on a bottle of pop.

Bevan hammered on the door once more. She lifted the letterbox and hollered, 'Mrs O'Driscoll! Mr Hadley!'

There was no response.

They'd come mob handed. Dani glanced down the road at the rest of her colleagues who were knocking on every door. One of the neighbours seemed to be at home, so the DCI stepped over the low hedge and joined DS Boag on the step.

'I've not seen either of them for a couple of days,' the young woman was explaining.

'Are they out at work during the day?' Phil asked.

'Mrs O'Driscoll is, but I'm not sure about her son. He comes and goes at all hours.'

Bevan could tell this was a bone of contention. 'Do you know where Mrs O'Driscoll works? It's a matter of some urgency.'

The neighbour screwed up her face. 'She's a barmaid at that big old pub down on the green. I can't remember what it's called. It's the kind of place you'd never dream of going into unless you were a total hard case, if you know what I mean.'

Dani glanced at Phil. 'We passed it on the way here.' They jogged towards the car. 'Thanks very much!' The DCI called over her shoulder, but the woman was already inside.

With the handful of local kids scattered to the pavements, leaving battered bikes on their sides in the gutter, the procession of police vehicles accelerated fast out of the estate.

Dani got on the radio and called for all available cars in the area to congregate at Neilston Green. Up until this point, Bevan hadn't been allowing herself to contemplate what they might find. But now, several nightmarish images were forcing their way into her mind. The DCI opened the passenger door and jumped out, before Phil had even brought the car to a proper standstill. 'You go round the front,' she commanded.

As she kicked open a door leading into the back of the run-down building, Bevan saw DCs Clifton and Mann sprinting across the grass to join her. She didn't stop to wait. With a hand on her baton, Dani stalked along a narrow corridor. It was fitted with a thick, brightly patterned carpet which masked her approach perfectly.

She was coming up to the bar area from the rear. A rowdy group of men were leaning on it, waving notes and waiting impatiently to be served. Bevan could only make out one person on her side of the counter. The barmaid was smallish, with a mass of unnaturally dark curls. Dani assumed this was Orla, which meant that Liam could be anywhere nearby.

A noise made Bevan turn her head. She noticed a door slightly ajar halfway along a corridor running at right angles to the one she was in. Dani unsheathed her baton and strode towards it. By this time, Alice and Dan were by her side. The DCI paused for a moment and then indicated to the others that she was going in.

There wasn't much light. Dani assumed they were in the cellar. She stumbled down the last few steps, having to right herself when she reached the bottom. 'Andy?' She called out gently.

It took several minutes for their eyes to adjust to

the darkness. It was DC Clifton who reacted first. He'd seen the outline of a large figure in the far corner of the basement, bending over an unidentifiable bundle on the floor. The detective bolted, landing a blow from his baton on the back of the man's head. Hadley pitched sideways, falling almost as if in slow motion, like a felled tree.

'Get some cuffs on him!' Dani yelled, heading straight for the lifeless figure lying on the cold ground. She skidded towards Calder on her knees, desperately ripping the tape away from his mouth and feeling his wrist for a pulse. 'His vitals are weak, but he's alive. Get the sodding paramedics down here pronto and arrest that bloody woman at the bar. No one leaves this godforsaken shit hole until I say so!'

Chapter 55

Orla O'Driscoll was in the interview room with the duty solicitor. Her son was still being treated at the infirmary. Liam Hadley was suffering from a suspected concussion.

DCI Bevan knew the PACE clock was ticking but she wanted the SOCOs to lift as much evidence as they could from the basement before she spoke with either of them.

Phil had stayed at the pub. Dani's phone started to buzz in her pocket. When she saw it was him, she picked up immediately. 'What have you got?'

'The pub cellar is definitely our murder site, for one of the victims at least. According to the brewery who own the place, Orla's been the acting manageress for over six months. She's had the run of the dump. They barely have enough clientele to justify any more staff than her and her son.' Phil cleared his throat. 'There are traces of blood all over that corner where Andy was kept and not all of it is fresh. The SOCOs also found some, err, instruments. Handles of garden tools that the techies reckon were used to penetrate McLaren.'

Dani took a deep breath, trying not to imagine what would have happened to Andy if they hadn't got there when they did. 'Do we think it was Orla or Liam who performed the sexual assaults on their victims?'

'It's impossible to say at this stage, Ma'am. That's going to have to be one for the interviewers and the shrinks.'

Her job, in other words.

Bevan ended the call and began walking towards

the interview suites, feeling as ready as she ever would be.

'Ma'am?'

Dani stopped in her tracks. By the tone of Alice's voice she knew it wasn't good. Bevan turned to face her detective constable. 'What is it?'

DC Mann's expression was stricken. Tears were flowing unchecked down her cheeks, although her voice remained steady. 'That was the hospital. Caitlin didn't pull through. She passed away from her injuries a couple of hours ago, whilst we were raiding the pub.'

Dani moved forward swiftly, taking the young detective in her arms before Alice's legs buckled beneath her. 'Come on, let's get you some tea. You've had an awful shock.'

*

After managing to swallow down a few sips of sweet tea, Alice looked a little better. 'She was only twenty-two.'

'I know,' Dani muttered. 'And she was on my team. I seconded her to my division for God's sake. I should have protected her like I would my own child.'

Alice shook her head. 'It happened off duty, Ma'am. Whatever Dan says, it was all Caitlin's idea to try and flush out the killer. In the end, all we did was enjoy a couple of nights out on the piss. If Dan and Caitlin hadn't seen Liam Hadley down that alleyway, DC Calder would be dead now. Murdered in the most horrible way imaginable.'

'One day that might make me feel better, but it doesn't yet and it won't for a very long time to come.'

Alice tried a thin smile. 'You know, it was DC Hendry who cracked this case. She was the one who found out about the O'Driscolls and their travelling fairground. She was convinced that there would be a link between the fairground operators that were working on the Glasgow Green on those Saturday afternoons and the murders. Caitlin was absolutely right. According to the Tax Credit database, Liam operates the fairground rides now for the larger, independent companies. He does all the big events like the Glasgow Fair.

Maybe he saw Nathan McLaren talking with his brother that afternoon, or he'd targeted him even earlier. Liam is good looking and charming, the temptation for Nathan McLaren to agree to meet him later that evening would have been too much to resist.'

'So Liam was the bait. Don Calder must have met him when he was interviewing ex-travellers about being evicted from their sites. Then he bumped into the man again when he took his kids to the Glasgow Fair. They must have taken a moment to exchange numbers, agreed on a rendezvous later that evening, perhaps.'

'But what was the motive, Ma'am? What did Orla and Liam have to gain by luring these men into their domain and then murdering them?'

Dani stood up and straightened out her skirt. 'It's about time I went to find that out, Detective Constable Mann.' The DCI set her mouth in a grim line. 'Wish me luck.'

Chapter 56

The first thing that Calder saw when he opened his eyes was the Gandalf lookalike guy standing at the end of his bed. He shifted to one side and identified DCI Bevan sitting in the chair beside him, her hand resting on his arm.

'How are you feeling, Andy?'

'My head hurts.'

'You took quite a battering. You've got a couple of broken ribs, but no permanent damage. Carol and Amy are in the cafeteria. They've been here all night. Shall I call them back in?'

Andy shifted himself up as far as he could, the effort making him wince. 'No. I want to hear what you guys have got to say first.'

Dani smiled. 'I thought you might.'

Professor Morgan cleared his throat. 'I hope you forgive my intrusion. Danielle asked me to sit in on the police interviews. The DCI thought I may be able to explain things to you more clearly than she could.'

'Who was the woman?' Andy demanded impatiently. 'Did she kill Don?'

Morgan held up his hand. 'It's perhaps best if I start at the beginning.' He pulled a chair up to the bedside. 'Orla Mary O'Driscoll was born into a family of showmen travellers. She was believed to possess the 'second sight' and therefore given the role of fortune-teller when they set up their fairground during the summer season. Orla was a beautiful young woman and attracted much attention from the other men in their community. At only 16 years old she married another traveller called Colm Hadley, who was in his early twenties. Hadley was an entertainer and magician, although the popularity of his act was on the wane even back then, forty years ago. Orla became pregnant very quickly and gave birth to a son, Liam.

But their marriage was not a happy one. Colm was often away, claiming that he was performing around the country at end of the Pier shows and local theatre houses, making some cash for the family. Orla was left to bring up the boy pretty much single-handed.

The O'Driscoll's were resident at a travellers' community to the south of Glasgow. They'd been at the site for generations. Liam was able to attend a local school along with the other traveller children. One day, Orla was sick and she stayed behind at the camp whilst the others set off for the coast to work the fairground. Orla went to see one of her elderly aunts, who provided the community with advice and medication.

When she returned to the caravan, Orla heard odd noises from inside. She was frightened. The woman recognised her husband's voice and thought he was being attacked. She wrenched open the door, discovering Colm on the bed with a young man. They were both naked and performing an act together that she could not comprehend.

Orla fled from the scene. Colm had hastily dressed and come looking for her. He told his wife that his desire for other men had no bearing upon their marriage. He said that if she wanted his support for Liam she would simply have to put up with it.

This was exactly what Orla did for the next few years. Colm was still often away from the camp but when he showed his face, she turned a blind eye to him bringing young men back to their caravan. As time went on, it became increasingly difficult to shield Liam from his father's lifestyle.

Then, after five years of living with Colm's proclivities and tolerating his adultery, there was a tragic accident.

One of the men who Orla's husband brought back to their caravan must have lit a candle. In their carnal reverie, they didn't notice that the wax had melted away to nothing and the flame was licking at the wooden table top. Within a few minutes, the caravan was engulfed by fire. Both Colm and his lover were killed.

Orla stood in front of the inferno and watched them burn. She and Liam were taken in by relatives. They struggled financially for a while. Then the widowed Orla O'Driscoll met a well-dressed businessman on the seafront at Wemyss Bay. She was still a young woman and very attractive. Michael Lomond began an affair with Orla and paid her money on a regular basis. She became pregnant by Lomond and gave birth to a little boy called Anthony, who lived with her and Liam at the travellers' camp.

Michael continued to support his son, but when it was clear that he and his wife would not be able to have children of their own, Lomond proposed to adopt Tony, his own flesh and blood, to bring up as their child. Orla was to receive a significant sum of money for the transaction and readily agreed. After all, it would give her youngest the chance of a decent life.'

'He looked like Tony Lomond,' Andy muttered, 'the man who kidnapped me. He was like an older version of Lomond.'

'They were only half-brothers, but the resemblance was very strong, as you say. Now, in their interviews, Orla and Liam's stories differed. Orla claims she loved her sons and would do anything for them. She suggests that Liam's hatred for his real father had developed at an early stage of his life. Colm was often absent, but when he did come home, matters were even worse. Liam was aware of his father's penchant for young men and it appalled him. According to Orla, by assisting him in killing his victims, she was helping Liam to assuage his anger towards married men who were practising homosexuals.

The first individual that Liam identified as a victim was poor Douglas Ross, a gentle man with homosexual tendencies, who had never acted upon them. Tony had told his brother the rumours about Ross. Then Liam met him on the beach at Wemyss Bay.

Hadley sought the schoolteacher out again and began a flirtation with him. Liam was handsome and intelligent. The day that Ross claimed he was looking for precious stones on the shore, he was meeting Hadley, on the promise that their relationship would be consummated. But Orla and Liam were waiting for him. They drugged the man before taking him to their house. The pub cellar wasn't available to them back then. This was their first kill.'

'So where did Ross end up?'

'He's at the bottom of the Crawhin Reservoir, just like Alice Mann predicted. We've sent the divers down today,' Dani volunteered.

'Which leaves Don next.' Andy blinked his eyes, not sure whether or not he really wanted to hear. 'Go on then, tell me what happened.'

Chapter 57

'Sadly, we believe now there were others in between.' Dani looked serious. 'We're gradually getting all the information out of Orla and Liam. We are trying to give them the impression we know about all the murders. But it's a slow process.'

'In the case of your uncle,' Morgan carried on, 'the pattern was slightly different to the others. Donald Calder had been investigating the fire that broke out at the traveller encampment near Paisley. This caused him to look at similar incidents amongst the showmen community. Through his research, he came across the tragic case of Colm Hadley in the late seventies. Liam's name was mentioned in the newspaper reports. Don got his address from a contact on the council.

As soon as Liam met Don, he knew the man was attracted to him. Like Ross, your uncle had been battling to suppress his sexuality for years. Liam noted the wedding ring, as he always did, and identified him as a target.

Liam Hadley was working one of the fairground rides at the Glasgow Fair in 2005, when Coco's was still in operation. He bumped into Don that afternoon, when he was there with his children. They arranged to meet later on that night. The fact that Don's wife had a migraine provided him with the perfect cover.

By this stage, Orla was working at the pub on Neilston Green and having a relationship with the manager. DCI Bevan's team are in the course of tracking him down.' Morgan sighed. 'We believe that the basement where you were held was the place in which Don was killed.'

Andy closed his eyes, but the tears leaked out nonetheless. 'Tell me about McLaren.'

'Liam met Nathan McLaren though his brother. Tony wasn't aware of it but Liam often watched his younger brother when he was out on the gay scene. I suppose it was a way for him to procure his victims. McLaren was an obvious target for the pair, middle aged and clearly new to the lifestyle. We know from Paul Black's testimony, that McLaren had met Liam at the Oyster Bar a couple of weeks earlier.

On the day of the Glasgow Fair, Liam was working the fairground once again, this time cash-in-hand. Whilst Nathan was wandering around on his own he was intercepted by Hadley, who arranged to meet him by the Balgray Reservoir that evening.

According to Orla, they had transport problems on that particular occasion. Their old car had broken down. McLaren had to make his own way to the rendezvous point by taxi cab. Nathan was killed out there in the country park, down an embankment by the railway bridge, beaten, assaulted and suffocated with whatever was to hand. His body was stuffed into a plastic bin bag, no time to weight it properly, as the trains were still running, carrying passengers home from the city.'

'So the McLaren killing was a botched job?' Andy had regained his composure slightly.

'Yes, they were fairly sure the body would be discovered, sooner or later. In all the other murders the men had never been found. No one was even looking for a killer. But from now on, they knew they'd need to be more careful.'

'Making them dump the trophies that they'd taken from the other victims?'

'That's right. Hadley came back later on, when he had some transport. Liam didn't know there was a mesh barrier downstream at the weir. He wasn't aware that the evidence had been found until he saw the items on Crime Scotland.'

'That must have been an unpleasant surprise.' Andy glanced at each of his visitors in turn. 'Which one of those two bastards carried out the torture of the victims - the forcing of the men to swallow their own wedding ring and the penetration with objects?'

Professor Morgan decided to answer. 'At this point, our killers are both blaming each other. Orla claims that Liam is the person who needs to brutalize these men, to find an outlet for his rage against the father who betrayed both him and his mother.

Liam tells a different story. He admits that he beats the victims, but his version is that Orla is behind it all. She harbours a deep-seated hatred for men who marry women knowing they are homosexuals. She despises their lifestyle and the lies and pain they inflict on their families. Liam says it's her who tortures their victims, taking pleasure as she watches them choke on their wedding bands, heartlessly ordering her son to finish them off.'

'Who do you believe?' Andy watched the professor's face closely.

'In my humble opinion, I think it's Orla who's the mastermind. Liam claims it was his mother who set the fire in their caravan all those years ago. He says she placed the candle on a pile of papers, knowing full well her husband was enjoying his carnal pleasures in the connecting room. She locked the door and watched them burn, hearing the men's screams and doing nothing.'

Calder involuntarily shuddered.

Dani turned when she heard a noise at the door. 'It's Carol, shall I let them in?'

'Aye,' Andy said with a smile.

Bevan and Morgan slipped out, as Amy rushed past them and launched herself onto the bed. Andy cried out in mock agony then scooped the girl up in his arms and began to laugh.

Dani briefly caught Carol's eye, seeing her mouth the words, 'thank you,' just before they pulled the door shut behind them.

Chapter 58

It was overcast in the city of Edinburgh, which was good news for the runners. The air was crisp and cool. Dani woke up in the bedroom of her boyfriend, James, at his tiny flat in Marchmont.

She watched him sleeping for a while, knowing he would need all his energy for the day ahead. When he finally awoke, he pulled her to him, planting kisses on her lips and neck.

'What are the rules with marathons? Is it like a big match – no sex for days beforehand?'

'We've already broken that one, so what the heck, eh?' James rolled over so that he was lying on top of her, gently pinning Dani's arms above her head.

'She glanced at the bedside clock. 'Shit! You'd actually better get a move on.'

James declined his coffee and stuck to fruit juice instead. He'd showered and put on his running gear, minus the incredibly expensive trainers which weren't going on until they reached the starting line.

'Remember all your training,' Dani said, as if she were some kind of expert. 'If you experience any tightness or pain in your chest, I want you to stop.'

'Okay, boss. Got the message.'

'I'll be at the finish line with my camera, so make sure you give a big smile for Facebook.' Dani moved across and placed her arms around him. 'I am proud of you.'

'I've not done it yet,' he replied dryly.

'No, but you've worked so hard for this and I've hardly been much of a support.'

'Dani, never apologise for the job you do. Your

work saves people's lives. Look at all those families who can now bury their loved ones. It's a bit more important than me jogging around this old city. What's the latest on the trial?'

'Hadley and O'Driscoll are drip-feeding the Fiscal's office with information about their previous murders. I expect they are hoping to delay the trial for as long as possible.'

'The lawyers will be encouraging them to do that.' James' father and sister had both been leading defence advocates. He knew what he was talking about. 'But a guilty verdict is inevitable, with all the evidence you have. There's no sign of either claiming diminished responsibility?'

'No, they wouldn't get very far with it. Liam Hadley is also charged with murdering a young policewoman. He's going to get no mercy whatsoever from the justice system.'

James eyed her with concern. 'And so he shouldn't. Did you visit Caitlin's parents?'

Dani nodded. 'It was the most awful thing I've ever done. Her father gave thirty years of service to the force. For the first time, I wondered if it really is all worth it.'

He brushed his hand across her cheek. 'What was your conclusion?'

'The jury's still out.' Dani reached back for her coffee. 'At least we got some closure on the west London murders. Rhodri Morgan called me before I left Glasgow. They've identified a local councillor who was a frequent visitor to the children's home in Acton where Ian Cummings spent much of his adolescence. This man also inspected a youth detention centre when Cummings was an inmate. The Met checked his movements in the late eighties. He was in London during the times of each of the murders.'

'Can he still be prosecuted? Do the Met have enough to convince the CPS?'

'The man died seven years ago of cancer. It was an aggressive form. Apparently, he had a nasty end.'

'But no justice. How about Cummings – has he admitted there was an accomplice?'

Dani shook her head. 'No, Rhodri has visited him twice, but he refuses to give the man up.'

'Maybe there never was anyone else. Harry Kyle might have been mistaken. You've no more evidence than his altered testimony, given twenty five years after the event. It wouldn't hold up in a court of law. I can't see why Cummings would continue to take the blame, even when his protector is dead and buried.'

'These people develop an odd bond. Look at Orla and Liam. They are drawn together by the tragedy and pain of their lives, feeding off one another's evil. Even the wicked need something to believe in, to cling on to. With Cummings it's his loyalty to this man.'

James went quiet, looking unsure of himself.

'What it is?' Dani asked. 'What have I said?'

'It's just when you commented on people needing to believe in something. It reminded me. I'm not sure if you'll want to hear this.'

'Go on.' She started to feel uneasy.

'When you first mentioned the name of the woman who helped to kill all those men. I'd heard it before.'

'Where?'

'Orla O'Driscoll was the name of the medium who was at Dad's party. Do you remember?'

Dani felt her blood run cold. 'The fortune-teller in the summer house?'

James tried on a weak smile. 'I know, pretty unlikely hey? She must have seen the name on an old poster somewhere, from a fairground long ago. I'm certain it can't have actually been the same person.'

'How did your dad get hold of her in the first place?'

'It was Mum who booked the entertainment. She saw an advert in the newspaper. The wording was terribly old-fashioned but Mum thought it might be fun.' James noted his girlfriend's troubled expression and took her hand. 'It must just be a coincidence. I've probably got the name quite wrong.'

Dani nodded, allowing herself to relax into his arms. 'Yes, it must be a mistake,' she mumbled.

'Oh God,' James had glanced at his watch. 'We'd really better get going.'

*

The sun was trying to break out as Dani stood with the crowds at the finishing line on Prince's Street. She was watching the giant digital clock closely, knowing that if James was making decent time then he should be reaching the end quite soon.

Dani put on her shades so she could watch the runners more closely. A woman was making a sprint finish, practically falling into the arms of two young men, clearly her sons. They wrapped heat conserving blankets around her and solicitously offered her a drink. It was Jenny McLaren and her boys. The tannoy announced that she was one of the top five fastest women to complete the course.

Bevan felt happy for her. It was lovely to see the woman in the embrace of her sons. They all looked well. Dani decided not to go over. She'd leave them in peace. Instead, she scanned the road ahead, finally seeing James approaching at a steady pace. No sprint finish for him. Bevan still experienced an unexpected surge of pride, and something else – love, maybe? She pushed through the crowd to the line, shouting him on as he raised his arms in victory. Dani forgot all about the photo, rushing towards him and helping to support his weight as he half collapsed in exhaustion.

'Did I do well?' He managed to say between heaving breaths.

'You did very well,' she replied, and they walked arm-in-arm towards the finishers' tent.

*

©Katherine Pathak, all rights reserved 2015

If you enjoyed this novel, please take a few moments to write a brief review. Reviews really help to introduce new readers to my books and this allows me to keep on writing.
Many thanks,

Katherine.

If you would like to find out more about my books and read my reviews and articles then please visit my blog, TheRetroReview at:

www.KatherinePathak.wordpress.com

To find out about new releases and special offers follow me on Twitter:

@KatherinePathak

Most of all, thanks for reading!

© Katherine Pathak, 2015

≈

The Garansay Press